"ALL BARGAINS SHOULD BE SEALED AND I THINK NOW IS THE PERFECT TIME TO SEAL OURS . . ."

His very touch seemed to burn her as he placed a finger under her chin and tilted her head to look up into his eyes. Gently, he kissed her lips with a feather-light touch, and Holly felt a warmness start in her throat and spread all over her, leaving her trembling. She tried to step away from him, but he caught her arms, pressing his fingers into her flesh, his eyes blazing. Her breath seemed to stop and she was only aware of the rhythm of her heart. She knew he was going to kiss her again, and this time it would be no gentle caress. And she also knew that she was completely powerless to resist him. . . .

A World of Romance from SIGNET

Forecast for Love

KRISTIN MICHAELS

A SIGNET BOOK

NEW AMERICAN LIBRARY

TIMES MIRROR

PUBLISHER'S NOTE

This novel is a work of fiction. Names, characters, places, and incidents are either the product of the author's imagination or are used fictitiously, and any resemblance to actual persons, living or dead, events, or locales is entirely coincidental.

Copyright © 1981 by Kristin Michaels

SIGNET TRADEMARK REG. U.S. PAT. OFF. AND FOREIGN COUNTRIES REGISTERED TRADEMARK—MARCA REGISTRADA HECHO EN CHICAGO, U.S.A.

SIGNET, SIGNET CLASSICS, MENTOR, PLUME, MERIDIAN AND NAL BOOKS are published by The New American Library, Inc., 1633 Broadway, New York, New York 10019

First Printing, November, 1981

1   2   3   4   5   6   7   8   9

PRINTED IN THE UNITED STATES OF AMERICA

For
Mary Elizabeth Burke Long
who has weathered life's
storms for almost 90 years.

1

∿∿∿∿∿∿∿∿∿∿

Holly moved uncomfortably in a chair that was designed for relaxation, deeply cushioned and nicely fitting the contours of her slender body. Waiting and hoping for something you really want is a miserable experience, she decided.

Attempting to adjust her mind to the uncertainty of waiting, she looked across the reception area and through the glass doors. She could see her beloved Wichita Mountains in the distance, towering majestically over the valley that held Arrowhead, Oklahoma, in its bowl-like terrain. Bringing her gaze closer, she studied the giant carved stone sign: KOK-TV. Oh, how she wanted this job!

In a nearby office, station manager Drake Wimberly, a man she had never met, sat behind his desk, holding her application in his hands—and it seemed to Holly almost her life. The palms of her own hands were moist from apprehension.

Suddenly, from the inner office, a beautifully timbred, resonant voice boomed into the reception room. "Holly Meriweather? I'm looking for an authentic, full-blooded weatherman, not a Christmas forecast!"

1

Her breath drew in sharply. With a nervous hand she smoothed an imaginary wrinkle from the cuff of her tailored blouse. He would surely think that she was Christmas in July, dressed as she was in a brilliant red dress and snow-white top. Earlier this morning she had doubted whether to dress so brightly was a good idea, but Frances Strom, her youthful, young-at-heart grandmother, had insisted that she looked as delicious as a candy peppermint stick.

"You look darling," Fran had said. "That dress is perfect with your curly brown hair and copper-colored eyes. And no one would believe such a creamy complexion came out of southern Oklahoma."

"You're prejudiced." Holly laughed. "As for being a paleface, now that I'm home, a few treks in the mountains during this summer heat will take care of that. But right now, I just want to look attractive enough to be a television weathercaster."

Only now a man she had never met had branded her a Christmas forecast!

Defiantly Holly lifted her chin. Couldn't he read? Her qualifications were clearly and neatly written on the application. A degree with a major in speech, plus some drama experience in little theater. And thanks to lovable, drawly-talking Henry Olsen, retired Weather Bureau chief and family friend, she knew almost as much about weather as a meteorologist. It would have been better if Drake Wimberly had already viewed her audition tape, but she did have it with her in a soft leather attaché case that was large enough to hold the tape, a new weather-research book, and the weather vane that she was carving for Fran's new dollhouse. Holly had thought she could study a few pages of the book while waiting for her job interview. Hah! Who could concentrate?

She tried to reassure herself. Even though Channel 33 had a reputation for hiring only male "on-the-air" personalities, Drake Wimberly would not find anyone in Arrowhead more qualified. Nor anyone who cared more! Nothing was more important to Holly than weather forecasting and storm-safety precautions, because her mother and father had died in a tornado, when, with proper warning, their lives might have been saved. The memory was vivid even though she had been only four years old when it happened.

The wind had blown hard across the Kansas prairie. Then the rain and hail came sounding like baseballs hitting the sides and top of their mobile home. Her tall, handsome father had come in from work, his clothes soaked and clinging to his body. Suddenly the rain stopped and the wind calmed. Then came the loud, thundering roar that sounded like a freight train. The mobile home began to rock, and Holly's beautiful mother caught Holly in her arms and her father grabbed them both, pulling all three to the floor.

The next thing she remembered was opening her eyes in a hospital bed and seeing her grandmother and grandfather standing by her side. At first Holly had thought Fran was her mother. They looked alike, and Fran's hair had been dark then, above the same wide lavender eyes as her mother's.

"Thank God, she's alive," her grandmother said. By some miracle, she had been saved and had received only a mild concussion.

Her grandparents brought her back to Arrowhead, sharing their life and interests with her—Fran shared her doll collection and dollhouses, and her grandfather taught her to carve. Under their loving care, she once again became a happy, laughing child. And there was ruddy-faced, lovable Henry Olsen who taught her about weather forecasting.

Now Holly's heart steadied a bit as she remembered her first simple weather lessons when she was only six years old and the Weather Bureau had been her playground.

"When everything is calm and smoke rises vertically, what is the wind speed?" Henry would ask.

"Less than one mile per hour," she would answer proudly.

They played the game of weather questions at every opportunity, although as she grew older, Henry emphasized that weather was a challenging and capricious lover. An intriguing, tantalizing one, too, but someday a human lover would come first with Holly. She wished it could be Kurt Bronson, who had been, more or less, her steady beau since childhood. But for now, Holly wanted only to learn more about weather forecasting and put that knowledge to practical use.

Once again her chin came up. Let Drake Wimberly make fun of her name all he liked. If the job weren't meant for her, would there be this opening to the career of her dreams in her hometown, where she wanted to live?

A buzzer sounded, and Drake Wimberly's deep voice came over the intercom. "Please, send in Miss Meriweather."

Joyce Moore, the continuity director filling in for the receptionist, smiled in Holly's direction. "His bark is really worse than his bite," she said. "Please go in."

Holly returned her smile, instinctively liking this flaxen-haired, dark-blue-, almost navy-eyed young woman who walked with the grace of a ballet dancer.

Just outside the open office door, Holly heard a loud catcall whistle. She turned toward the sound with a withering glance to face a cold-eyed young man wearing while coveralls with the name "Nelson" embroidered over his breast pocket. A headset detached from its camera plug perched atop a thatch of unruly straw-colored hair. He looked much too forbidding to be giving catcalls, but there was no one else in sight. So it must have been him.

More amused than angry, Holly dismissed him from her mind, intent once again on meeting Drake Wimberly.

She squared her shoulders and walked into his office. He rose from behind his desk to greet her and moved to close his office door. He was tall, rangy, undeniably handsome in his western-type slacks and coat of soft brown suede. His shirt was open at the throat, revealing a gold medallion gleaming against his skin, browned as an Indian's. He surely must spend more time in the sun than behind a desk. A long, attractive mouth turned up at one corner as though constantly amused by something or someone.

"Miss Snowbird, I presume," he said, his eyes slowly going over her own clothes.

He was outrageous!

Holly stiffened and tried to react with an icy stare, but when her eyes met his hazel ones flecked with brown and gold glints, a strange feeling ran through her and she felt almost breathless. His face seemed to change, and she wondered if she saw approval in his eyes. An unfamiliar warmth enveloped her. Never had any man affected her at first sight so strongly. But she would have to be careful. This was no time to meet her White Knight, particularly not in the guise of a man she hoped would be her boss.

Briskly he motioned her to a chair, his desk forming a barrier between them. The moment was over, at least for him. Attraction? Recognition? Whatever, it was ended, although she was conscious of leftover tingles.

He looked at her application, then at her, almost sternly. "You seem well enough qualified," he said, and hesitated. "But I'm not at all sure you're what we're looking for." He held her gaze without flinching. "Frankly, I want an experienced weatherman, not a beginner."

"Weatherman?" she snapped, emphasizing the last syllable. "You must know you can't discriminate against me because I'm a woman." She should have known from all his male announcers that he was an insufferable chauvinist.

"Now, don't get your dander up. Weatherman, weatherwoman, I don't care. 'Experienced' is the key word."

Somewhat mollified, she replied, "But don't you see—"

He interrupted, "I see that our weather ratings are low. The other three television stations in our viewing area have us on the run in the weather segments."

"I have a number of good ideas for weather shows," she said firmly. "Teaching the viewers to do their own simple weather forecasting, for example. Just the way Henry Olsen taught me."

"You do have a super reference in Henry," Drake said thoughtfully. "We're both interested in converting wind to energy, and he's almost convinced me to join him in an experimental project when he finds the right location to generate, store, and convert wind power for practical use."

"He's a real nut on that, I know," Holly said. "Wind energy and his ideas that the South should have won the war."

Drake Wimberly chuckled. "I hadn't heard about that."

"I think he carries on about the Civil War mostly to tease my grandmother."

"We certainly have a mutual friend in Henry," Drake said. "His farm is just down the road from my place. Your home must be in the same area?"

Holly nodded. Now she knew why the Wimberly name had been familiar. Fran had written her during her first year in college that Jack Wimberly had died and his only relative, a nephew, had inherited Wimberly Hills with its thousands of acres of wooded land, ranching pastures, and oil wells galore. With all of that, why on earth was Drake Wimberly managing a television station?

Before she could ponder the inconsistency, Drake spoke again. "Let me look at your audition tape now. I owe Henry that much," he said. "If you do come across on camera, you would be very easy on the eyes of our male viewers. On the other hand, that might not set too well with the ladies."

Affronted in spite of his smile, Holly stiffened. "I assure you I'm interested in weather forecasting, not in attracting men."

"That is completely out of your control," he said in that infuriating, teasing way.

She felt her face redden, but before she could reply, there was a sharp knock on the door, then it opened. A tall, breathtakingly lovely woman with long auburn hair sailed into the office as if she owned it.

She ignored Holly's presence. "Drake, you simply must come to the studio," she announced imperiously. "Bryan says he can't do the bouncing ball for my First State Bank commercial."

"Bryan is the production manager and the director, Denise. You know his word is final as to what can and can't be done." Despite Drake's firm words, the deep resonance of his voice was soft and gentle. Curiously, Holly stared at the woman. Who was she to Drake that she dared barge into his office?

"Once the new board is installed, we can press a button and do all the bouncing balls you like," Drake said placatingly.

"But we did it before," Denise insisted.

"It was very amateurish," he replied.

Their conversation gave Holly an opportunity to look more closely at the office. The walls were decorated with modern graphics and an impressionistic painting that was to her nothing more than an abstract splash of color. She would have thought that Drake would choose wall hangings with more realism. Palette-knife paintings of mountains, and perhaps seascapes.

The other furnishings were ultramodern, too, but so much chrome and glass didn't suit Drake, she decided. However, from the way he smiled, ultramodern Denise certainly did. And this office was right down her alley, judging from her fashionable black pantsuit, its gold-nail-head trim calling attention to the way the suit clung seductively to her willowy body.

"You can at least come to the studio to help us decide what to do," Denise said, her voice demanding immediate action.

"Of course," he agreed. "I want to see Miss Meriweather's tape anyway."

He introduced the two women. Holly wasn't really surprised to learn that Denise Warren was a one-woman advertising agency. She looked the part. And it was quite apparent that Denise was accustomed to having things her way.

"So you want to do the weather," Denise said, appraising Holly carefully. "If you get the job, it will be well for you to remember that without commercials, there would be no weathercasts."

Holly turned to Drake, expecting him to say something about the importance of weather shows. Instead he only laughed and patted Denise affectionately on the shoulder. Holly felt like an intruder and left out of something she couldn't name. One thing she knew intuitively. He would make certain that Denise's dilemma was settled and that she was happy before he bothered to look at Holly's audition tape.

2

Holly took the square box from her attaché case and handed it to Drake Wimberly. Suddenly her heart was racing. Inside the box, the piece of video-tape, looking like nothing more than a wide black ribbon wound on a large spool, would determine her future. It seemed strange that she had made it before a camera in a television production studio in Dallas more than two hundred miles away. This innocent-looking piece of black material, when threaded onto a huge black machine, could reveal on a television screen the way she had looked and the things she had said.

Drake Wimberly took the videotape from her and suggested they adjourn to the studio. They walked together down the long hall and turned left into a door marked "Control." It was a long narrow room with one wall covered in a line of metal cabinets, filled, Holly knew, with transistors and tubes and all the things engineers worked on almost constantly to keep the equipment working and a picture intact to be transmitted to home television sets.

The technical director sat on a raised platform in front of a board full of buttons to be punched at the proper time. Holly had a great respect for anyone with a mind nimble enough to think fast and almost automatically press the right button for Camera One, Camera Two, or whatever, all the while quietly giving instructions to the floor crew in the studio.

Just above the director's board at eye level were several monitors that looked like ordinary small television screens placed side by side. With a flick of his finger on a button, the director could see on the monitor what each camera was focused on. Another monitor showed the activities on network, and yet another revealed the picture going out on the air from Channel 33's transmitter.

It's a fascinating world, Holly thought as the three of them walked up the steps to the platform. Through a large expanse of glass she could see that the stagelike platform overlooked a square studio for live telecasts and for videotaping. The news and weather sets were in one corner, but other backgrounds for commercials and live programs other than news were put up and taken down as needed.

Holly's conjecture was correct that Denise's happiness was of first importance. After Holly was introduced to the production manager, Bryan Simmons, Drake handed Bryan the videotape.

He said, "We want to see Holly's audition tape,

but first let's take a look at the bank commercial without a bouncing ball."

Bryan cocked an eyebrow and winked at Holly. She smiled at him and knew she would be comfortable with this calm blue-eyed young man. He wasn't as tall as Drake, but he had a lankiness that made him look taller. He walked slowly, almost deliberately, and Holly had the feeling that it would be impossible to rush him. He explained patiently that Denise wanted a bouncing ball over the notes and words on the music staff of the bank's singing jingle.

"But I want to bounce the ball over the entire spoken message, too," Denise said.

"We simply can't do it until the board is ready," Drake said.

"Then what do you suggest?" Denise asked icily. "I like to work at this station because it's more convenient, but I could have done the commercial in Wichita Falls." There was a menacing tone to her voice.

"You surely wouldn't run a commercial for an Arrowhead bank on a Wichita Falls station," Drake said.

"Of course not," she snapped.

"Then it would cost you a pretty penny for studio time, wouldn't it?" Drake asked reasonably. No matter what he said to Denise, Holly noticed again that his voice was patient and kind. Was he that way with everyone, or was Denise special?

But Denise was intent on a solution to her problem. "Then you come up with an answer!"

Drake turned to Bryan. "What do you think?"

The production manager shifted his lanky frame

from one foot to the other. His blue eyes were guarded, and when he spoke, it was in his slow and deliberate manner. "The jingle looks okay without the bouncing ball, don't you think? Why not do the middle part with an announcer on camera?"

"What announcer?" Denise retorted. "You know I don't like any of your announcers on camera, and I must get the commercial finished this afternoon." Holly, listening, wished ardently that a decision of some kind would be made.

Bryan shrugged his bony shoulders, and Drake looked pensive.

"Wait," Denise announced. "You want to see her audition. She can do the commercial." Denise pointed a finger toward Holly. Was there a triumphant "we'll-take-care-of-you" sound in her voice?

"We're not a big-city station, so doing commercials is a part of the job," Drake said to Holly.

She felt anger rising inside her. It wasn't fair. She had worked hard to get a good weather audition tape, and now they expected her to step in front of the camera and do a commercial cold when she'd never in her life done one before.

On the verge of refusing, she became aware that the others concluded that the problem was solved. She must do the commercial.

Holly sat on a high stool at a counter and studied the copy while the straw-haired cameraman put the words for her to say on the teleprompter. She had found out that the cameraman's full name was Nelson Sternum. Bryan, not rushing, but working steadily, directed the rest of the floor crew in setting up a desk and background for the commercial.

She stopped her study of the copy to admire the flat that was set up behind the desk to make the scene on camera look like a real office with a bookcase and even a window. Grudgingly she had to admit that it wasn't a bad idea for a woman to do the commercial. It was a message on women's services at the bank. She closed her eyes and listened to the words inside her head to hear how they would sound. She almost had the copy memorized when Denise walked over to the counter.

"I think I'll change the copy at the end," Denise said breezily, taking the paper from Holly and penciling in the change. Was Denise trying to make the commercial more difficult for Holly to do?

"Here it is—just a better bank in a better town, First State and Arrowhead," Denise said. "You'll have to remember it, because the copy is already teleprompted."

Holly stiffened. I'll show you, Miss Advertising, she said to herself. I can do this commercial and any others you bring around.

"Okay, let's go," Bryan called across the studio.

Drake gave her a good-luck sign as she sat down at the desk. Intently she repeated the copy change several times. It would be easy to muff the end when different words appeared on the teleprompter. Then the red eye on top of the camera lit up.

"Stand by, tape's rolling." Nelson Sternum relayed instructions from Bryan, who was now in the control room and talking through the headset.

Then the cameraman pointed a finger at Holly,

signaling her to start the message. She was through the thirty seconds before she realized it, but she had no idea how the commercial looked or sounded.

"Good," Drake said. "I think we have a take."

Holly breathed a sigh of relief, but Denise spoke, very businesslike. "I'd like to do it again. She needs to emphasize 'a better bank in a better town.'"

Holly thought she had done so, but nonetheless the commercial was done again, not once more, but three more times. At the end of the third go-round, Holly knew she had lost all feeling for the words. If one of the first two wasn't good enough, she knew that her audition tape wouldn't save her.

But everyone agreed that the first take was the best, that, in fact, it was excellent. Everyone agreed except Denise.

She spoke crossly. "I just can't spend any more time on this, so I suppose it will have to do." She turned to Holly. "I'll get your address from Drake and mail you a check."

"That won't be necessary if she goes on the payroll," Drake said. "Her charge is included in the studio time."

Holly's heart sang at his words, but Denise's eyes widened. "You're going to hire her?"

"If her audition tape is good, we'll give it a try," he said, and then turned his hazel eyes on Holly. "If that's all right with you."

"Oh, yes," Holly replied fervently, her pulse pounding both at the thought of getting the job and from Drake's warm glance.

He looked at his watch. "It will be a while yet before I can look at your audition. Suppose I let you know tonight or tomorrow?"

She hoped her disappointment didn't show on her face, but she consoled herself with the knowledge that the commercial would be used and that her audition tape was professional. Surely the television weathercaster's job was hers. But why couldn't he just go ahead and look at the videotape?

In answer to her unspoken question, he explained, "It's almost four o'clock, and our videotape machine will be tied up with the network news feed."

She must have still looked puzzled, because he continued, "Each day at four o'clock the various networks telecast world and national news to their local television affiliates for the stations' use on local newscasts."

She thanked Drake, trying to conceal her disappointment, and was turning to leave the studio when Bryan called to her. "Perhaps you'd like to watch part of the news feed," he said. "A film loop comes down, too, of all the weather-satellite pictures from NOAA."

Holly knew about NOAA. National Ocean Graphics and Atmospheric Administration, a real mouthful that had been shortened to NOAA and pronounced as one word. Easy to remember, also, because Noah in the Bible was associated with weather.

As she followed Bryan into the videotape room, he explained that the film loop showed satellite pictures taken from seven P.M. at night until seven A.M. the following day, and another that ran from seven A.M. until noon. "The entire film loop comes in Monday through Friday at four o'clock except on holidays," Bryan concluded.

Holly knew that when bad weather was developing, satellite pictures could pick up something only four miles in diameter and that it took local radar to tell when to duck.

Another man that Holly recognized as Hal Fitzgerald, the news director, was in the videotape room waiting for the news feed. He was stocky and solid-looking, and when she watched him on the news, she was impressed with his quiet, sincere delivery. He appeared to have that same quality in person that he had on the television screen.

His piercing black eyes kindly but firmly measured her. "Do you live in Arrowhead?" he asked.

"I grew up here and I hope to live here again," she said, and smiled. She told him that since her graduation from college two years ago she had worked at temporary secretarial jobs in Dallas, waiting for a chance to do weather forecasting for television.

"Drake wants me to look at your audition tape with him," Hal said, "and word has already drifted around that you did a good job on the bank commercial."

Holly was pleased, but before she could reply, the news feed started. The weather-satellite pictures showed fair weather, except for rain along the Atlantic coast. After watching the film loop, she decided it would be best for her to leave and wait for Drake Wimberly's call. She said her good-byes, but as she was going out the door, she failed to see the straw-haired catcalling cameraman until they collided.

"Careful there, your Royal Highness," he said, obviously still smarting from her earlier visual rebuff when he had whistled at her outside Drake's office door.

"Just a moment, Miss Meriweather." It was Drake Wimberly's voice, very stern, very formal. She turned to face him.

Again his eyes appraised her, this time with no warmth. "Just a word of warning if you get the job." His eyes were steely, with none of the teasing glints she had already grown to expect. "We have no room for limelight-hunting prima donnas. A sense of humor, I might add, helps."

How unfair! He certainly had lost *his* sense of humor. Was it just the incident with Nelson Sternum, the cameraman, or had Denise said something? True, a few television personalities were temperamental, but he had no right to judge her. She had a few labels of her own for Drake Wimberly!

Arrogant. Condescending. That should be plenty. If she hadn't wanted the television weathercasting job so badly, never would she have considered working for such a man!

3

Holly sped away from the television station in her gold Pontiac Sunbird, cheeks burning with hurt and anger. Through the side-view mirror she watched the rough-hewn stone building disappear as she rounded a curve in the road, but she could still see the tall television tower with its huge dish transmitting television programs. Would it never carry her weathercasts?

She felt her anger fading, replaced by a quaking in the pit of her stomach. *If she got the job!* Drake Wimberly had emphasized the "if" as though he had a big doubt. He had approved the commercial, she reminded herself, and surely he would like her audition tape equally well. But Denise Warren hadn't really been pleased, so would she influence him not to hire Holly?

She wished it were earlier in the afternoon. She could drive the short distance to the mountains and walk through the trees she loved, watch the birds, quail and highland plover, maybe see a deer or an antelope.

It had been so long since she'd been to the mountains. There had been no time in the few days she had been home. In the past, whenever she was troubled, the mountains never failed to bring her peace. She was grateful that the Wichitas had been turned into a wildlife refuge. Even now, just seeing the range in the distance eased her nebulous fears.

On an impulse, Holly bypassed the turn homeward and continued driving toward town. She might not have time to visit the mountains, but she could spare an hour to visit Kurt. She was sure he would still be in his office. At this moment she needed the approval Kurt was certain to supply.

She pulled the Sunbird into a parking space just as he walked out of his office. When he saw her, his face broke into a delighted grin, and he ran toward her car with the same speed that had made him a good football quarterback. His gray eyes and light brown, almost blond wavy hair had created the perfect gridiron hero. Holly liked the way his nose wrinkled when he laughed, spotlighting the sprinkle of freckles that made him seem much younger than he was. In spite of his appealing boyishness, he was a shrewd and very successful businessman, already head of his own insurance company.

He hurried to open the car door. "Just thinking about you," he said happily, warming her heart after the shock of Drake Wimberly's parting remarks. "Let's walk over to the Regency Club for a drink."

"A quick one" she said, falling in step beside him.

He took her hand as they walked the half-block, then through the revolving door into the hotel and across the lobby to the oak door that led to the club. The atmosphere was elegant and quiet. Kurt chose a secluded area for two with comfortable leather swivel chairs at a small round table. Others might join them at the longer tables with the plush couches against the wall. He ordered Scotch and water, but Holly, realizing that she hadn't eaten since breakfast, decided on a nonalcoholic version of a Bloody Mary.

"A Virgin Mary." Kurt smiled.

Whatever it was called, the crunchy celery stalk in the pepper-hot tomato juice was satisfying the gnawing hunger that for the moment had replaced all other feeling. But she acknowledged to herself that even the intense and sudden hunger was really caused by her fear that something—or someone—would prevent her going to work at Channel 33.

"Alone at last," Kurt said companionably.

"But not for long," Holly replied. "Fran won't be at all happy if I'm not home in time for dinner. She'll want to know what happened at the television station."

"I had forgotten that you had the interview this afternoon." Kurt took a gulp of his drink. "If the job will keep you in Arrowhead, I hope you get it. What was the verdict?"

She recounted the afternoon, finishing with, "I just have a feeling that Denise Warren might try to influence Drake Wimberly not to hire me."

"Was he that smitten with you?" Kurt asked, his eyes narrowing.

She colored. "I didn't mean . . . I didn't even like . . . Oh, Kurt, don't tease me. This is too important."

"I wasn't teasing," he said quietly.

"Drake Wimberly isn't interested in me, nor I in

him," she said heatedly, then took a sip of her drink and ate the last bit of the celery in a deliberate attempt to cool her indignation. But her voice was still cross when she spoke. "Since I was ten years old, you've thought every male within shouting distance was interested in me."

"But not very often have I thought you were interested," Kurt said softly. "You know how I feel about you, and, yes, I've been jealous many times." His face was so strained that Holly wanted to reach over and smooth the frown lines from his forehead. "But you know, sweetheart," he continued, "if you married me, all that would change. I wouldn't be jealous anymore."

She felt a tenderness toward him, but she almost knew that it would never be anything more. "I'm not ready to think about marriage," she said. "Not to you, nor anyone. Maybe one day I'll feel differently."

"And maybe you won't," Kurt said glumly, motioning to the waitress to bring the check. "What will you do if you don't get this job?"

"Look elsewhere, I guess." It was Holly's turn to sound glum. She continued talking as they left the club and once again walked through the revolving hotel doors out into the deepening shadows of the late afternoon. "I do want to stay here. Since Grand Ben died, Fran is all alone."

Holly saw Kurt smile at her childhood name for her grandfather. When she was a child, it had been Grand Ben and Grand Frances.

Kurt took her hand again as they walked slowly toward her car. "From the rumors I hear, Fran isn't alone very much," he said. "Henry Olsen is around quite a bit."

"Of course he is. He builds the dollhouses for Fran's doll collection."

"Are you still carving the weather vanes?" he asked.

The mention of weather vanes jogged her memory. "My attaché case, where is it? The weather vane I'm working on is in it."

Holly rushed toward her car, leaving a puzzled Kurt behind. Hurriedly she looked inside the car. Kurt caught up with her as she rummaged under the seat. "I've left it at the television station."

"I'm sure it will be safe," he said.

"It does have my name stamped inside. But since tomorrow is Saturday, the front offices will be closed."

"Pick it up Monday, then," Kurt said, kissing her softly on the cheek as he helped her into the car.

"But I wanted to work on the weather vane this weekend so that it would be ready when Henry finishes the new dollhouse," she fretted. "It was stupid of me to leave the attaché case."

"Since you won't be carving, have dinner with me tomorrow night."

Holly didn't miss the look of longing in his eyes, but if she didn't get the job, she knew that her mood would be too gloomy for dinner with Kurt. "Call me tomorrow," she said.

How simple life could be if she married Kurt and forgot her dreams of being a television weather forecaster. She drove slowly along the boulevard lined with pecan and oak trees. Just before she turned

onto Center Road that led home, she noted the
clouds of spread-out vapor trails above the crimson-
and-gold sunset.

With no organized wind direction at the cloud
level, she felt that the present quiet weather would
continue. But would her own inner weather tomorrow be turbulent or fair?

Topping a low hill, she felt a rush of wincing
nostalgia at the sight of the picturesque scene in the
valley. The familiar redstone gable-roofed house,
scattered outbuildings, and a sweep of emerald
meadow all rose before her as she descended the
slope. She found the break in the roadside hedge
and turned the car into a drive that was nothing
more than a narrow graveled path amid a profusion
of plants, flowers, and a vegetable garden. Beyond the riot of summer squash, tomato plants, and
various flowers she could see the iron gate in the
white picket fence that surrounded the lawn of
green grass.

Holly pulled her Sunbird in behind Fran's blue
Buick. The other two parking spaces were occupied
with Henry Olsen's ancient but serviceable salmon-
colored Chrysler, and beside it, a four-wheel-drive
Ramcharger. She frowned, more concerned at facing
a stranger inside the house than who the stranger
might be.

For a moment she was tempted to turn her car
around, have dinner at a roadside café, and call
Fran that she had been detained. But the chance
that Drake Wimberly might call was too overwhelming. She didn't want to miss that call.

Resolutely she squared her shoulders, practiced a

smile, and stood before the double doors. In the brightness provided by the porch light, her eyes were drawn to the niches that resulted when, very young, she had tried to carve a bird's image into the door. The incident had led to her first carving lesson.

"Never carve on anything that is already beautiful," Grand Ben had said. He started her carving on soap, showing her how to hold the knife so that she wouldn't cut herself. Finally she graduated to soft wood and carving the weathercocks for the dollhouses.

She couldn't stand here gazing at the door forever, so she took a deep breath, picturing the scene inside the door and off the hall into the den with its high-beamed ceiling and old-fashioned fireplace.

Fran would be curled up little-girl fashion at one end of the brown velvet couch, the one contemporary touch in an otherwise traditional room. Henry would be relaxed in Grand Ben's old reclining chair, most likely gazing into the liquid depths of his bourbon and "branch water," sipping only occasionally. Holly had known Henry's one drink to last an hour or two. And the stranger? Or strangers? Here her imagination ended. She would have to open the door.

Her eyes adjusted to the soft light in the wide hallway, drawn toward the stairway. Perhaps she could scurry past the open den door and fly up the stairs to the safety of her bedroom. Then she became conscious of the voices in avid conversation. Fran's soft lilting tones, Henry's deep baritone, and . . . Her heart literally tried to beat itself out of her chest. Once again she heard the beautifully timbred, resonant voice. It couldn't be, but it was.

Drake Wimberly!

4

ᴗᴗᴗᴗᴗᴗᴗᴗᴗᴗᴗᴗ

Holly entered the familiar room, and for a moment it was she who felt like a stranger. Henry stood by the fireplace and Drake sat in Grand Ben's chair. He had leaned forward a little, speaking to Fran.

"With wind power, it's the movement of air around the earth that averages temperature extremes. And it's that air movement that produces the surface winds used for power generation," he said.

Did he always assume ownership of any place he happened to be? Holly wondered. He appeared to be perfectly at home. She was overwhelmed again by his rich-looking clothes and his impressive physical attractiveness. With his beautiful voice, he should be in front of the camera, not behind it.

Holly came closer, and Fran saw her. A glow of excitement gripped her. With both hands Fran held up Holly's attaché case. "Look, your new boss has returned your belongings," she said.

New boss? Had she really gotten the job? Breathless, Holly turned questioning eyes on Drake.

His own hazel eyes were teasing. "When possessions are left behind, I've heard it's because the person expects to return." Drake grinned. "Were you really that sure you had the job?"

His words were discomfiting, and Holly didn't know how to reply. Embarrassed that she had been so careless, she managed an outer calmness. "I only hoped," she said, "but you needn't have troubled yourself."

"No trouble," he said smoothly. "I did want to let you know that you had the job, and returning your satchel was only a half-mile off the track on my way home."

She really had the job. He had just said so. She wasn't sure that she could contain her happiness. She wanted to dance and twirl about the room, but the others would probably think she should accept her good fortune with a little less exuberance.

Drake spoke again. "You failed to mention on your application that wood carving was one of your talents."

A faint tone of disapproval in his voice relegated wood carving to the eccentric category. Once again Holly felt defensive. But she was saved from replying when Henry handed her a goblet of white wine.

She smiled and thanked him, taking the drink. She reached up and kissed him on the cheek, hoping he knew that her thanks was for much more than the glass of wine. His ruddy face grew even pinker and his eyes twinkled with pleasure.

Drake's voice drew her attention back to him. "I told Fran and Henry that you did quite well on the commercial."

Fran? How quickly he developed a first-name relationship. But then, she had to admit that friendly and outgoing Fran was a first-name kind of person.

Fran uncurled from the couch and popped to her feet, her full peasant skirt twirling about her legs that still looked as if she ought to be a hosiery model. "Congratulations, darling," she said. "With a teacher like Henry, how could you fail?"

Surprised at the tenderness in Fran's voice, Holly watched her grandmother's velvety lavender eyes linger lovingly on Henry. Kurt could be right. Something more than an old friendship seemed to be under way. Sweet mystery of love, maybe someday it would come to her.

The look that Henry returned to Fran was so full of longing that Holly felt embarrassed to be watching. She turned back to Drake and saw hidden laughter bubbling from his eyes, the corner of his mouth turning up in a smile. Was he making fun of her grandmother and Henry?

Holly stiffened and took an involuntary step to come between Drake and the two older people. She looked at him, intending for her gaze to say: *You will not spoil this moment. Not for them, not for me!*

But when she looked deeply into Drake's eyes, her heart quickened and her body began to tremble the way it had when she first saw him. Was it really only several hours ago? It seemed much longer. *I am in control of my mind and heart,* she said to herself silently. This man was to be her employer, only her employer and nothing else.

When words finally formed, her voice was husky

and low. "I appreciate the chance and I'll work hard. You won't be sorry you hired me."

"We'll see," he replied noncommittally. "I'd like for you to start work on Monday." His voice was businesslike and detached. "You'll do your scheduled commercials, then get ready for your six-o'clock weathercast. Then take a supper break and back to the station in time to get ready for the ten-o'clock run."

Henry walked over and put his arm around Holly, raising his glass in a toast. "Here's to beauty and brains all in one small dynamite package, just like your grandmother." The room seemed to vibrate with love and goodwill. "To your success, my dear."

Fran and Drake joined Henry in the toast, but when Holly's eyes met Drake's over the rim of his glass, she saw the warning. She was sure he was telling her to watch her step, that she was only on trial.

Would this man always cloud her moments of triumph and happiness? Defiantly she whirled away from him and sat down on the couch.

Drake didn't seem to notice her abruptness, or if he did, he chose to ignore it. Following her to the couch, he sat down beside her. Really, why was he still here? Now that he had hired her, surely it was time for him to be about his plans for the evening. With Denise Warren or someone equally glamorous.

He must have sensed her question, for he said, "Your grandmother has enticed me to stay for dinner, aided by Henry's glowing words about her fresh-vegetable quiche, salad, and corn on the cob."

"Which will be served in just five minutes," Fran said, heading toward the kitchen.

Holly literally jumped from the couch. "With my help, it may take even less time."

She was eager to be away from the overwhelming physical presence of Drake Wimberly, if only for a few minutes. Quickly, in three trips, she and Fran had transported the food to the big dining room with its buttermilk painted brick walls, heavy ceiling beams, and balloon-shaped draperies of green, apricot, and yellow floral on a white ground. A bordered area rug in white covered the parquet flooring. And the bronze-and-crystal chandelier completed the formal country scene. As they sat down at the oval dining table, Holly thought how justly proud Fran was of this room.

Holly stole glances at Drake as he sampled the quiche. Her own slice was delicious, with succulent bits of broccoli, cauliflower, carrots, and mushrooms cut up in small pieces, and carrying just a hint of garlic.

"Marvelous, Fran," Henry said.

"It is, it is," Drake echoed. "Would you give the recipe to me?" he asked eagerly, almost boyish in his enthusiasm.

"I'll copy it for you immediately after dinner," Fran replied. "Nothing pleases the chef more than to be asked for a recipe."

Drake laughed. "Just try asking Manuel for the ingredients in his enchiladas."

"You must eat at Manuel's, Holly," Fran said. "It's a new Mexican-food place on Travis Hill."

Holly murmured that she would like to, and was glad that she had not been called on for more than a comment or two. It was just now really dawning on her that she would actually be working at KOK-TV. Despite the deliciousness of the food, she was only nibbling. The excitement was growing too much for her to eat.

"What kind of cheese?" Drake asked, still interested in the quiche.

"Ricotta. Half a cup of ricotta and half a cup of grated Swiss cheese. Occasionally I've tried cottage cheese, but it's much better with ricotta," Fran insisted.

For the moment, Drake appeared to have forgotten Holly, intent on enjoying his food. Suddenly she was aware that a question had been directed to her.

"Well, Holly, can you come, too?" Drake asked.

"Come where?"

Her reply brought gales of laughter.

"Already she is at work," Henry said.

Fran spoke. "Drake has invited us to a barbecue tomorrow afternoon at Wimberly Hills. Henry and I have accepted."

"I'm sorry, I had drifted away." She hesitated. "I half-promised Kurt to go to dinner."

"One of your many boyfriends, I presume," Drake said.

"You presume wrong," she said, realizing instantly that her voice was snappish. She mellowed her tone. "Kurt is a friend, yes. A childhood friend."

"You don't have to explain," Drake said amiably. "Bring him along."

"Thank you, I'm sure he would like that," Holly said formally.

"Then it's settled. I'll expect you tomorrow at four." They finished dinner and began to move toward the den. Drake said, "I really must leave this lovely gathering." He suggested that Holly walk to the gate with him to clear up any questions she might have about her new job.

Fran quickly wrote out the quiche recipe for Drake and handed it to him as he and Holly walked out the door. "And do remember," Fran admonished, "to sauté the onion and garlic until tender, but not browned."

Walking down the path toward Drake's Ramcharger, Holly realized that she was very tired. Darkness had cooled the breeze, and she took in long breaths of the sweet-smelling air. The sky was star-filled and light from the full moon spread a misty halo over the countryside.

"Nowhere but Oklahoma," Holly said appreciatively.

"A Texan might argue with you," Drake said.

She looked at him questioningly. "I grew up in Texas," he explained, "in a little community near Abilene. Ranch country with miles and miles of flatland with sunrises and sunsets you wouldn't believe." His voice was soft and dreamy. "No mountains like the Wichitas, but with its own brand of beauty."

Holly was touched at his loving description. Why, he could be almost human.

They were at the gate, and Holly reached for the latch, feeling the coolness of the iron. Drake put his hand over hers and pulled it back. His touch seemed to burn. Then he put his hands lightly on her shoulders. His fingers sent little shots of electrical currents through her body.

"All bargains should be sealed," he said, "and I think now is the perfect time to seal our bargain."

He moved one hand from her shoulder, and with a finger under her chin, tilted her head to look up into his eyes.

Gently he kissed her lips with a feather-light touch. Holly felt a warmness start in her throat and spread all over her, even to her toes. It left her trembling. What would happen if her really kissed her?

"Till tomorrow, little Spirit of Christmas," Drake said, and without a backward glance moved toward his Ramcharger. She stood watching the curls of dust that could be seen from the taillights.

When Drake was out of sight, she returned to the house, bid Henry and Fran a fond good night, and walked up the stairs to her bedroom. How good it was to be here in this room where she had grown from a child to a young woman. The green and rose colors made her feel good. The draperies with their rose background were drawn, concealing the small gallery outside the sliding glass door. The wallpaper matched the draperies, and the walls were trimmed in raspberry. There was a deep green velvet slipper chair and a chaise in dusty rose. In the Queen Anne mirror gilded with green lacquer, she looked at her reflection and saw that her copper eyes were glistening from the excitement, like a newly minted penny. Beneath her bare feet, the rose-colored carpet felt deep and plush.

Gratefully she climbed the bed steps onto the carved four-poster bed and sank deliciously into the deep comfort, wondering what kind of bargain had been sealed.

Was it just working for Drake Wimberly, or was there something deeper? Suddenly a sense of foreboding came over her, and she shivered. Tired as she was from the day's events, sleep would not come.

With her arms embracing the pillow and lying on her stomach, she could feel, even hear, her heart beating with a staccato drumbeat rhythm that seemed to be asking a question. *What is happening to me, happening to me, happening to me?*

5

It was early morning when she opened her eyes, aware that she must have slept, for she remembered—it must have been a dream—she remembered two hearts beating. Her own heart . . . and had the other heart been Drake's?

She must *not* think about that. It was enough that her entire life had changed. Holly couldn't remember a time when she hadn't avidly watched the television weathercasts, putting herself in the weathercaster's place. In her mind, it was she, her body and her voice, that came from the television screen.

And now it was to actually happen, no longer

pure imagination. But perhaps in every dream come true there was a stumbling block. Drake Wimberly affected her far too strongly.

Swinging her feet over the bed to the bed steps, she scolded herself. *Forget it!* Now was the time to concentrate on the career she'd dreamed of, prove she could be good at it.

She didn't want a romantic interest at this time, particularly not a romance with the man who was to be her boss. She tossed her head in a decided manner. Anyway, Denise Warren very likely had her stamp on him.

Holly changed her nightclothes for a pair of jeans and a soft terry top, intending to get a cup of coffee from downstairs and bring it back to drink on her gallery. She loved to sit there in the open air and look out at the mountains, sometimes working on her carving. She walked over to the sliding glass door and looked out. A misty purple haze shrouded the mountains, gilded by the first rays of the morning sun.

She bounded down the stairs for the coffee. But Fran was there prancing and dancing around the kitchen like a teenager. Hmmm, Henry, no doubt! True, Fran's first words were about their old family friend.

"Henry is proud of you, almost as though he was solely responsible for your getting the job," Fran said, her voice pausing tenderly when she spoke his name.

Holly smiled. "In a way, he is, love," she said. "Without Henry, I would never have had my weather background, and Drake Wimberly has great respect for him." She couldn't help but notice the dancing lights in Fran's velvety eyes. She continued, "Do we have a romance going here?"

"I'm sure from the way Drake looked at you—"

Holly interrupted, "You know, dear, I meant you and Henry."

Fran's blush was answer enough. "At my age?" she said.

"Your age." Holly laughed aloud. "You with your dolls, dollhouses, and the way you gad about like a teenager."

"Anyway, Henry treats me like an antebellum belle. I'm sure he'd like for me to wear hoop skirts. I'm just too independent for him."

"I have a feeling that can be worked out," Holly said confidently.

Fran dismissed the subject with a wave of her hand. "Bring your coffee along," she said, "I want to show you the new doll."

They walked together out the back door and traveled the covered walkway to Doll Heaven, a sizable log cabin that housed the dolls and dollhouses. It was built away from the house so that doll lovers could, by appointment, come browse and sometimes buy the dolls that Fran could bear to sell. Children often came, too, to be enchanted.

The phone extension in Doll Heaven was ringing when Fran opened the door. It was Kurt, so Holly relayed Drake Wimberly's invitation. Kurt was delighted. "What I wouldn't give to latch on to a sizable chunk of his insurance!"

She rebuked a twinge of annoyance, knowing that his constant lookout for new prospects was the very trait that made Kurt successful. Nonetheless, she resented his trying to turn social occasions into opportunities to pick up insurance business. She hoped he wouldn't embarrass her with any such attempts at Wimberly Hills.

Holly pushed her concern about Kurt's behavior to the back of her mind so that Fran could show her the latest doll acquisition. It was another Ginny doll. True, it was a modern doll, but Ginnys were becoming scarce. This one, Fran told her, was made in 1962, a fifteen-inch Ginny with jointed waist and sleepy blue eyes. Fran now had a complete set of the dolls that were forerunners of "family" dolls. Eight-inch Ginette, ten-inch Jill, twelve-inch Jan, and a taller Jeff, who was the brother or boyfriend.

"I love the Ginny dolls," Fran said. "Jennie Graves, their creator, 'dreamed of Ginny' and made that dream a reality. She was left a widow and supported her children with her doll business." Fran's eyes were alight with admiration as she spoke. "I always remember that Jennie Graves overcame all sorts of adversities, turned necessity into opportunity, and made countless little girls happy at the same time."

"Another American success story." Holly laughed teasingly. She remembered her own childhood and the many delightful hours she had spent here. The dollhouses, first made by Grand Ben, later by Grand Ben and Henry Olsen, became more and more realistic. Now Henry even illuminated them with tiny battery-operated lights. Fran's love of dolls must have been one reason she stayed so young and vital.

However, that recent love light in her eyes had nothing to do with dolls.

"Oh," Holly exclaimed, "here's one I haven't seen." She picked up a closemouthed doll with a face of porcelainlike bisque, big brown eyes, perfect eyebrows, and a lacy bonnet over realistic brown hair.

"A Jumeau French doll, sister to the openmouthed French dolls," Fran explained. "I've named her Michelle. Isn't she beautiful?"

"Expensive, too, I imagine," Holly said.

"Very," Fran emphasized.

Holly waited for Fran to find just the right spot for her new sleepy-eyed Ginny. Finally she was free to return to the house, pour another cup of coffee, and head for the gallery off her bedroom. Upstairs in her bedroom, she gathered up the unfinished weathercock, her carving tools, and the lap board that was her worktable, carpeted to keep the wood from splitting.

Opening the sliding glass doors, she stepped out into the morning air and sat down in a comfortable lounge chair. The gallery was protected from the sun, so although it was midmorning, it wasn't yet too warm for Holly to relax and be surprisingly content to simply carve with only an occasional bubble of excitement to interrupt her inner quietness.

As she carved, she remembered that Grand Ben had insisted that Jesus of Nazareth was not a carpenter, but a woodcarver. The word translated "carpenter," he said, actually meant an artisan. Grand Ben was a wealth of information on many subjects, so Holly suspected he was correct when he told her that during biblical times wood was too scarce for anything except interior decoration and carving.

"You should treat the wood with respect," he would say. "The wood you are cutting has probably lived longer than will anything you can make of it." He had taught her to select her woods carefully. A delicate piece such as her weathercocks needed a close-grained wood, and apple wood was a good choice.

Holly was working on the head of the weather-cock when the telephone rang. Fran must have been out of earshot, for it continued to ring, so Holly put her carving aside to answer it on the telephone beside her bed.

She spoke breezily, "Good morning."

But the tone that came from the other end of the line was anything but cheery. "I'd like to speak with Drake Wimberly, please!"

Holly was sure she recognized Denise's voice, but she said, "I beg your pardon?"

The female voice repeated her request. Yes, it was Denise. "You must have the wrong number," Holly said. "This is the Strom residence."

"I know it's the Strom residence," Denise snapped. "I saw Drake turn in to your place not more than fifteen minutes ago. The name 'Strom' is printed clearly on the mailbox."

"You must be mistaken," Holly answered firmly. "Since he's throwing the barbecue today, I'm sure you'll find him at home."

"I'm calling from his house," Denise replied haughtily, then paused before she spoke again.

"Miss Meriweather, you must surely know that Drake will not like your lying to me."

"Oh, for heaven's sake," Holly said, unable to control her exasperation. But Denise probably hadn't heard that remark, because she had hung up the phone.

What could possibly be the purpose of such a phone call? Was Denise trying to tell her something? Holly shrugged, looked at the clock, and saw it was noon. She realized she hadn't had breakfast, but remembering the heavy food she would be eating later today, decided she would fix only a light lunch. She gathered up her carving material from the gallery, put it away, and walked down the stairs.

At the bottom of the flight, Holly met Fran just coming in the front door. "How about a tuna-fish salad?" Holly asked.

"Sounds great," Fran replied. "You just missed Drake Wimberly."

The two were walking toward the kitchen, but Holly grabbed Fran's arm and gasped, "Drake?"

"He was in a hurry and didn't want to disturb you," Fran explained. "Henry had given him a map to look at a location for their wind-power generator. That was before you came in last night. Drake had left it on the chair-side table."

Holly was appalled. Now she would have to apologize to Denise. She told Fran about the phone call.

"Serves her right," Fran said. "You did say she wasn't at all complimentary about the commercial you did, yet Drake and everyone else apparently thought it was great."

"Maybe not great," Holly demurred.

"Anyway, it appears to me that she has her eye on Drake Wimberly and is already jealous of you," Fran concluded.

"That's ridiculous," Holly said, but inwardly shivered, remembering his gentle kiss and the way she had felt.

"He does look at you as if you were his favorite flavor of ice cream." Fran paused. "Anyway, I can't imagine that he's the kind of man who would enjoy being tracked down everywhere he goes."

Maybe not, thought Holly, but would she ever be able to convince Denise that she hadn't deliberately lied? Holly didn't look forward to the apology she must make.

After lunch, she cleaned her bedroom and bath, then helped Fran downstairs with a kitchen scrub-up and furniture polishing. The time passed swiftly, and before she knew it, it was time to dress. Kurt had promised to be there at four "on the dot." Despite her leisurely day, she would have to rush to be ready.

After a quick shower and rubdown with a huge towel which left her skin tingling, she went to her closet and chose a new western outfit that she had worn only once, a navy denim prairie skirt and frontier shirt of cotton chamois, the front and back yoke outlined in fringe. With the costume, she decided to wear her comfortable beaded moccasins instead of boots.

Fran announced her appearance smashing. "The perfect candidate for an Indian love call," she said, "but I somehow doubt that you'll be answering Kurt's."

"I'm not answering any love call," Holly replied firmly.

"Not even Drake Wimberly's?" Fran teased.

"I'm sure I won't have to make that decision," Holly said, but felt another pang at remembering the night before. That would have to stop. She tried to joke. "Probably he's already answered Denise Warren's signals."

"We'll see," Fran said as Henry's double staccato knock was heard.

"Now, that's a love call," Holly said with a laugh, but she wasn't sure Fran heard, so eager was Fran to get the door open and greet Henry.

The laughter faded inside Holly, changed to a wistful longing. It should be enough that at last she would have her chance to forecast weather. But she had to admit, despite her resolves, that she was beginning to think of Drake much more often than she should if she meant to keep her mind on her career.

6

The pensiveness clung to Holly even after Kurt arrived, walking unsteadily in his cowboy boots. But by the time the four of them piled into Henry's Chrysler for the short drive to Wimberly Hills, she was getting her good humor back and was caught up in the festive mood.

She even laughed aloud when she decided they looked like escapees from a western-movie set. Fran in western jeans, cowboy shirt, bright bandanna scarf, and cowgirl boots. Henry, as usual, in complete cowboy attire, including a wide-brimmed Stetson hat that shaded his ruddy face. Kurt looked like the banker in a western movie, the dressed-up version of the western gentleman with a flat-topped fuzzy hat.

"It's ermine," he said proudly, removing the hat to pass it around for inspection. Holly returned it to him quickly. She wasn't all that crazy about small furry creatures being killed to make a hat.

Henry's car rumbled over the cattle guard and turned into the wide tree-lined lane leading to the stately house and grounds of Wimberly Hills. Holly watched eagerly for her first glimpse of the big house at the top of the hill, almost tree-shaded from view.

It was similar in style to Fran's house, the same gingerbread carvings on the eaves of the house, but much more mansiony, with touches reminiscent of European castles. Where Fran's house had only one gallery off Holly's bedroom, the Wimberly place had two private balconies on the second floor.

But the main attraction for Holly had been the third-floor tower. She had been there once when she was only about ten years old. Raising her shoulders and lifting her head to what she had considered a stately height, she had walked up the winding stairs to the tower. The round room was lined from floor to ceiling with books that she had been told spilled over from the library downstairs. For Holly, it had been for the moment her castle, and she was a princess. She had looked out at the Wichita Mountains, peopled in her imagination with brightly dressed soldiers marching off to battle to defend her country.

She smiled at the memory as Henry rounded the turn at the foot of the hill. Cars were everywhere, but Henry quickly found a parking space. As they got out of the car and walked up the hill, the gentle wind wafted the sounds of western music. Holly wasn't surprised that Drake had hired a band. He appeared to be a person who did all things in a big way. Did that include love?

The four of them were soon engulfed by the milling crowd. Fran and Henry stopped to say hello to a group of people they knew, but Kurt was heading Holly toward the beer kegs. She stopped to watch the couples dancing on the concrete patio and to look for Denise. She wanted to get that unpleasant chore out of the way.

"I'll wait here, Kurt," she said.

"No beer?" he asked.

"No beer," she said firmly.

At first she saw no one she knew, but then she spotted Nelson Sternum, the straw-haired cameraman, dancing clumsily with a blond, who looked bored. And no wonder, thought Holly, almost giggling. She'd bet that Nelson was stepping on the blond's toes about every other beat of the music.

Then Holly saw Drake and felt a deadening thump inside of her when she saw that his partner was Denise Warren. Her apology to Denise would have to wait. Drake was holding Denise closely, smoothly keeping step to the plaintive strains of a ballad of a lover who wanted his sweetheart to release him. Apparently the two were only listening to the melody, not the words, because Denise clung to Drake as if she would never let him go, and certainly Drake didn't seem to mind.

They even looked like partners, with Denise wearing an emerald green satiny western costume that was almost identical in color and texture to Drake's shirt. Denise and Drake. Even their names went together with a rhythmic emphasis.

Sadly Holly took her eyes away from the engrossed couple. People shouldn't make such a public display of feelings, but she reminded herself that what Drake Wimberly did was none of her business.

Although she had told Kurt she would wait for him at the edge of the dance floor, she walked on. Wandering a short distance away from the crowds, she leaned her back against a big oak tree and closed her eyes to steady herself. She breathed deeply and for a moment became almost oblivious of the laughter, the buzz of conversation, and the music. She didn't know how long she had stood there drifting toward an inner serenity when suddenly she felt a soft kiss on her eyelid. Startled, she opened her eyes, expecting to see Kurt. Instead, she looked into the teasing eyes of Drake Wimberly.

"But you were dancing," she stammered.

His voice was gentle. "And now I'm here to remind a pretty girl that closing her eyes in public is dangerous. It arouses the male animal."

"I was just . . . oh . . ." Once again he had managed to leave her at a loss for words. How inept he could make her feel!

"It's a good party," she said lamely, her heart still hammering.

"The secret of good parties is to invite interesting people," Drake said. He paused for a moment and then said, "Now it's your turn to tease me."

"Tease you?" Holly said, puzzled.

"For leaving the map behind, indicating that I wanted to return," he said.

"Did you?" she asked, hoping her words came out teasingly and not breathless, the way she was feeling.

"Of course," he said, "and I'm sorry I missed you."

Holly grimaced, wrinkling her nose and forehead. "I must apologize to Denise for telling her you hadn't been there."

"That won't be necessary, since I've already told her that you didn't know I had stopped by," he said.

Holly was relieved, but she couldn't help but note in her mind that Denise had wasted no time in telling Drake.

"Come, let me introduce you around," he said.

She followed him as he began the introductions, a sea of names and faces she was sure she would never be able to remember. She did recognize the name of Dr. Bill Carlson, a courtly gray-haired gentleman who seemed to be chewing on the cigar in his mouth rather than smoking it. Several years before, he had removed Fran's appendix. When he was young, he had wanted to be an opera star, and Fran had told her that he swore he had sung *Rigoletto* during her operation. Holly could tell from the twinkle in his eyes that he did have a good sense of humor.

After meeting Dr. Carlson, they walked over to a picnic table where Bryan Simmons sat with Joyce Moore. She really should have been a ballet dancer, Holly thought, for she even managed to look graceful sitting on a picnic bench. Holly was also instantly aware that here was another romance. Joyce's blue, almost navy eyes were sparkling and adoring on Bryan, while he responded with a tender gaze. Both almost reluctantly turned their attention to Drake and Holly. Someone called Drake's name, and with apologies he left them.

Then Bryan spoke. "I'll leave you two to girl-gab while I get a beer." He pulled his rangy body from the picnic table and asked if he could bring them anything.

"Nothing," Holly and Joyce replied.

Joyce watched him slowly move away before she turned to Holly. "You're going to be a great asset to the station," she said. "We're all delighted that Drake is willing to change the all-male image that Jim Carstairs established."

"Jim Carstairs?" Holly was puzzled.

"The previous manager," Joyce explained. "Drake fired him amid Jim's threats of bombing the station and general mayhem."

"He wasn't serious, surely," Holly said.

"We don't really know. He did try to break up some equipment before he left. But the police arrived and politely ushered him out. We found out that he went to work as manager of a radio station in Wichita Falls. Too close for comfort."

"And Drake didn't have him arrested?" Holly asked.

"No, Drake is really one of the good guys of all time," she answered fondly. "Too bad he'll only be manager until he can find a capable replacement. After all, he has his ranching and oil interests as well as owning the television station."

Holly's heart sank at the thought of Drake's leaving the station. True, she had told herself over and over that her mind was closed to romance, but her heart sang a different song in spite of the fact that Drake and Denise had rhythmic names.

We sealed a bargain, she wanted to cry out. Unreasonably, she felt betrayed. Determined that her feelings wouldn't show, she tried to smile brightly.

"I'm sure it's better for the television station to have someone familiar with the business at the helm," she said.

"I doubt it," Joyce answered glumly. "From the moment Drake bought the station, he started learning the ins and outs. He's made a real study of the business from the engineering end to sales." Joyce paused, gracefully changing her seating position. "Of course, he has a degree in marketing, so that helped."

Holly made no reply, but she was aware that Joyce was studying her closely. She hoped her face wasn't readable, for out of the corner of her eye she had seen Denise Warren walk over to Drake and slip her arm possessively through his. "Let's dance, darling," Holly heard her say. "The band is playing our song." Holly identified a country-western version of "Somewhere My Love."

Joyce heard Denise, too, for she said, "Watch your step with Denise. She is viciously attached to Drake and has made it clear that she'll get rid of any female who tries to infringe." There was an ominous note of warning in Joyce's voice, and Holly was painfully aware that Drake's and Denise's look-alike clothes told the world that they belonged together.

"She'll have nothing to fear from me," Holly said with determined emphasis.

As if to prove her statement, Kurt appeared and Holly introduced him to Joyce.

"I couldn't find you," he said accusingly to Holly, his boyish face taking on a stern look. She noted that the sun seemed to have popped out an additional freckle or two on his nose.

Holly reached up and kissed his cheek, glad for the opportunity to show Joyce that she had her own interest.

"We haven't danced, even once," he said.

"You two run along," Joyce said. "I'll find Bryan."

Holly tensed as they two-stepped across the dance floor, feeling smothered by Kurt's closeness. She was relieved when the band started playing a fast tune and she could excuse herself from dancing.

Once again Kurt headed for the beer keg. Holly stayed behind, watching him elbow his way through the crowd around the keg and then emerge with a mug full of beer, foam overflowing and sloshing to the ground. She saw him head toward Drake, who was talking with a group of several people that included Henry and Fran. *Please*, she sent him a mental message, *don't start in on your great insurance plans.*

With a sigh, she turned and walked toward the house. Drake had told everyone to feel free to roam the house. For a little while, she wanted to be alone to sort out her feelings. She stood for a moment in the hallway, breathing in the quietness.

Holly walked past the parlor on the right and library on the left. The sliding oak doors on each side were closed, and she hesitated to open them. But just beyond, the combination dining/sitting-room doors were open.

What a magnificent place to dine! It reminded her of morning sunlight with the brightness of yellows and blues. And yet despite the comtemporary colors, it was still traditionally elegant. The dining table was small, but it could be extended, she knew, with several leaves. The Chippendale dining chairs were covered in yellow leather. There was a tall stripped pine vitrine filled with objets d'art.

In front of the fireplace was a black settee with decorated finish, upholstered in yellow, cream, and blue stripes. Close by was a comfortable-looking wing chair in navy-blue moiré. She doubted that Drake had done the redecorating, but nonetheless the room revealed his good taste.

Almost without taking thought, she mounted the spiraling staircase leading to the tower room. Drake had mentioned the "comfort station" on the third floor, so she knew he wouldn't mind a guest's being there.

The tower room was the same motif she remembered. It was a "chromoscape" of color, with berry-red walls, plum woodwork, a mirrored wall, Oriental rug, and a Florentine fireplace. Holly had forgotten that fireplaces were in almost every room. A sectional sofa was covered in a patterned canvas fabric. In addition to bookcases against the wall, interesting photographs, blown up as art, hung on the other walls. A marvelous room for just sitting and thinking. Suddenly she heard the sound of birds and realized the chirping was coming from the fireplace chimney.

She looked from the window at the scene below—people everywhere. Food was being spread out on long tables. Barbecued chicken and beef that had been cooking, she was sure, in the pits all day, to a mouth-watering tenderness. And there were German potato salad, red beans, and tons of green salad. The food looked delicious, but she was in no hurry to eat.

Beyond the scene below, Holly could see the sun hanging like a crimson ball above the mountains.

"So you've found my ivory tower."

Holly jumped as if her hand had been caught in the cookie jar, but his voice was so gentle, she relaxed. How Drake Wimberly must love the time he spent here!

Turning slowly from the window to face him, she could picture him stretched out before the fire reading a book, dark outside, with only the sounds of logs crackling and rain beating against the windowpane.

She drew in her breath as she imagined being with him on such an evening, then shook her head slightly to erase the image from her mind. She tried to replace it with Denise Warren at his side, but somehow Denise didn't seem to fit this room.

She grasped for something to say. "You have birds in your chimney," she said, but didn't intend for the words to sound accusing.

Drake smiled. "Chimney swifts. They build their nests in the chimney, and I leave them there because it would kill the baby birds if I had them cleaned out." He appeared to be embarrassed at showing such tenderness for small creatures. Certainly this was a side of Drake Wimberly that Holly hadn't suspected.

"They fly with incredible speed," he said. "I've watched them sometimes diving like bombers into their nests with unbelievable accuracy."

"I'm sure the birds are grateful to you for not disturbing their home," she said, trying to keep her voice light.

Abruptly, still seeming slightly embarrassed, he changed the subject. "You haven't danced with me. May I claim the first dance after dinner?"

"Of course," she said, realizing her voice was prim. But could she stand the closeness of dancing with him?

His eyes gentled even more than when he talked about the birds. "You look so right here," he said. "When I interrupted you, were you a queen in your tower, looking out upon your subjects?"

"Queens get beheaded." She laughed shakily. "No, the one time years ago when I was here, I was a princess and the soldiers were going to battle to defend the country, and perhaps my honor."

He took a mock menacing step toward her. "From such reprobates as me?" he asked.

Holly felt a blush spread over her body. "I . . . I didn't know you then."

She turned to step away from him, but he caught her arms, pressing his fingers into her flesh, his eyes blazing. Her breath seemed to stop, and she was only aware of the rhythm of her heart.

He was going to kiss her, and she knew it would be no gentle caress like the last time. But she was powerless to resist. Then, as suddenly as he had seized her, his hold loosened and she was free. She was shaking. From relief or disappointment?

"I . . . I was looking down at the food, realizing that I'm famished," she said. She had to think of some way to get away before she completely crumpled into his arms.

She was saved by the sound of Denise's voice calling for Drake.

"I'm here," he said, looking toward the stairway and back to Holly. "Perhaps it would be better—"

Holly interrupted, "Of course." At least she had stopped trembling, but she knew he meant that it would be better if Denise didn't find them together.

To protect her? She doubted it. More likely he knew that Denise would cause a scene if she found her man alone with another woman.

She watched Drake walk down the stairs to meet Denise. Then Holly descended slowly to the bottom of the stairs and quickly left the house. Drake and Denise were nowhere in sight. Perhaps they had slipped into one of the rooms in the house for a love scene. It was none of her business, she told herself firmly, but it didn't help when she heard the band playing "Born to Lose."

7

Holly's face was so rigid that she felt it was cracking as she moved among the guests, trying to smile as if she were having a good time. She would look for Kurt, then make a pretense of eating a plate of food, and perhaps by that time it wouldn't be too early to suggest that they leave. She doubted that Drake would remember he had asked her to dance. He was still nowhere in sight, nor could she spot Kurt. But she did see Nelson Sternum, just finishing his food and sitting alone at a small table.

She walked toward Nelson's table. It might be a good idea to join him and let him see that she was not as uppity as he seemed to think.

"How's the food?" she asked brightly.

He looked at her sourly, and she could tell it would take more than a friendly overture to get him to warm up. "Food's food," he commented. "Good or bad, it all goes to the same place."

She didn't quite know how to reply to that, so she simply smiled. She stood for a moment while he looked at her with an inscrutable expression on his face. Hesitantly she sat down at the table.

While he didn't object, he certainly wasn't responding to Holly the way most men did. Her face felt hot, and she took a paper tissue from her bag to wipe away the beads of perspiration. She was annoyed that she had made any effort at all toward this dour cameraman. It wasn't necessary that everyone in the world find her an interesting companion.

He was looking past her, his face screwed up into a mass of wrinkles, his lips set sternly. She turned around to follow his gaze and saw Kurt talking with Denise a short distance away.

"People take advantage of her," he said almost sadly.

"Denise?" she asked incredulously. He must know a different Denise than she'd encountered so far.

Before she could speculate further on Nelson's strange remark, Kurt had left Denise and joined Holly.

"You are the most disappearing female I've ever encountered," he said, but there was a smile in his voice. Holly was glad that, at least, Kurt was in a good humor.

Trying to match his lightness, she said, "I just wanted to see if you would miss me."

"Sometimes you're even gone for years," he said teasingly. "Try it again and I'll just forget you."

She was beginning to feel better with Kurt's familiar banter. "I'm hungry," she said, although she really wasn't. But going for food would get them away from this table where Nelson was still intently following Denise's movements. Holly and Kurt left him with a cordial farewell, but he only waved his hand in recognition of their leaving.

Kurt followed her as she selected her food. Just a

bite of potato salad, a spoonful of beans, and a small hunk of barbecue was all she placed on her plate. But she did take a sizable portion of green salad in a separate plastic bowl.

"Surely that's not enough potato salad," Kurt said, and spooned a large helping onto her plate. She didn't protest, although she knew it would go uneaten.

They joined Henry and Fran, both of whom were bathed in halos of radiance, resulting no doubt from dancing closely together. It was a bright spot in the afternoon just to see the two of them so happy. Once Holly started to work as a television weathercaster, she would be equally contented, surely. It was this job she wanted, not a romance. Nevertheless, she looked about for Drake, half-wishing for and half-dreading her dance with him, if he remembered.

But he came up behind her, and she didn't see him until he spoke. "May I dance with Holly?" he asked Kurt almost formally.

Kurt nodded his assent, and despite the heat of the late afternoon, Holly felt an inner nervous coldness as she walked with Drake toward the patio. With so many guests enjoying their food, the floor was less crowded than it had been.

She drifted naturally into Drake's waiting arms, but blushed when she realized the music hadn't started.

"Who needs music when two hearts can beat as one?" Drake said into her ear, holding her close. Too close, for he surely must feel her trembling. But then the music began and Holly surrendered to the rhythm of Drake's body and his sure guidance as they moved around the floor.

The band was playing a song she had never heard. "May I have this dance with you for the rest of my life?" the lyrics said. She was lost in the melody, in the lightness of her steps and Drake's moving together. His closeness now seemed natural.

This is the way life should be, Holly thought, feeling her heart lighten and lift. A feeling of security and rightness took hold of her. She never wanted this time to end.

But the moment was over and she descended from her heaven, though she smiled into Drake's eyes with a look that surely must tell him how much she enjoyed the dance.

"One more time," he whispered, and once again she moved into his arms. But the band who had helped create the mood just as surely now destroyed it. The musicians began a loud and vigorous polka.

Drake shrugged, looking down at Holly. "Let's try it anyway," he said.

She nodded, wishing the Bohemians had kept their special dance. They joined the other dancers, hopping and skipping around and around. The dance floor became more and more crowded as the guests finished eating.

In the whirl of faces, Holly saw Nelson and Denise together. It was hard to tell who was leading whom, because Denise obviously was intent on getting closer to Drake and Holly. Denise kept watching them and inched nearer and nearer. Over and over, the dancers took a hop and three small steps in fast double time. The music increased to a frenzied pace. Holly saw the set, determined look in Denise's eyes.

Drake and Holly were in perfect step to the double-time music. Suddenly Holly fell with a thud to the floor. Stabs of blackening pain came from her ankle. Someone had tripped her!

Deliberately? Denise? Nelson? Certainly it hadn't been Drake, and Holly knew she hadn't simply lost her balance.

She was sure that a blow against her right leg had knocked her down. She had tried to hold on to Drake as she went down, but her fingers had slipped from his and Drake wasn't able to keep her from falling.

The dancing stopped as the couples gathered around Holly. "Stand back and give her air," she heard Drake say. "Will someone please find Bill Carlson?"

Through her agony, Holly remembered the silver-haired doctor she had met earlier. Kurt, Fran, and Henry were there now. Kurt tried to push Drake aside, but Drake stood firm, then crouched beside her and lifted her gently to a sitting position. "Don't try to get up," he said. Beneath the pain, Holly felt foolish and awkward.

"Let's get her inside the house." It was Dr. Carlson's voice. Kurt moved toward her, but it was Drake who scooped her from the floor into his arms, into the house, and gently lowered her small body onto the couch in the dining/sitting room.

"This may hurt," the doctor said as he examined the badly swollen ankle. He asked Drake to find a bath or kitchen sponge. Then Dr. Carlson turned to

Fran and told her to get a bucket of ice. The doctor explained that the best treatment for sprains was to apply direct pressure to the injury by using sponge rubber held in place by an elastic wrap or even adhesive tape. "Then it's best to apply ice directly over the part that hurts and elevate the leg."

After Drake returned with the sponge and Fran with the ice, the doctor handed Drake his car keys to bring his doctor's bag from the front seat of the car. "I have elastic wrap with me," he said, and grinned. "You never can tell when a sprained ankle will turn up."

"Are you sure it's not broken?" Holly asked timidly, her voice unsteady from the pain.

"Almost sure, but if it is, this type of treatment is helpful for sprain or fracture." The doctor's words were reassuring. "Most people think that fractures must have immediate care, but mostly this is not true." He turned toward Fran. "A fracture takes at least six weeks to heal, and provided there's no bone sticking through, it doesn't matter that much whether the bone is set immediately, tomorrow, or the day after."

"But how will we know?" Fran asked, her face showing concern.

Dr. Carlson finished putting the elastic wrap in place before he answered. "If the ankle isn't better by Monday, we'll investigate the fracture possibility." He patted Holly's arm. "Let's hope, if you stay off the ankle, you'll be much better in a couple of days. I'll give you a few pills to keep down the pain." He handed Fran a small packet, withholding a single pill for Holly to take immediately.

Fortunately Drake had produced an ice bag, and soon Holly felt a little more comfortable. She looked around at the concerned faces and saw Denise Warren moving toward her. Holly was aware that Denise looked less than sympathetic.

"It's really too bad that you won't be able to start work on Monday," Denise said, but she couldn't quite hide the fact from Holly that she wasn't sorry at all.

Holly felt a stab of pain that was from her heart and not her ankle. Not beginning her new job on Monday was unthinkable.

The doctor agreed with her inner thoughts. "Provided the ankle isn't fractured, she should feel like working by then," he said. "A pair of crutches would be helpful, though, for what moving around you have to do over the weekend and even on Monday."

Kurt at last could be useful. "I'll locate the crutches," he said. Then he looked toward Dr. Carlson. "How soon can we take her home?"

"Whenever she feels like being carried to the car," the doctor said. "I'm sure she'll be more comfortable in her own bed."

Holly smiled weakly. "I'm ready anytime," she said.

This time Kurt was not to be dissuaded. Quickly he moved to lift her carefully from the couch, but Drake walked beside them to Henry's car. Although it wasn't his fault that she had fallen, he said, "I'm so sorry. I can't imagine that I couldn't keep you from falling." Holly couldn't see his face, but she heard the tenderness in his voice. He continued, "It isn't necessary for you to start work on Monday."

Holly didn't say so, but she intended to be there if she had to crawl. When she was feeling less groggy, she would think through the events and maybe figure out who had tripped her and whether it had been on purpose or accidental.

By the time Holly was tucked safely in her own bed, she was too drowsy from the pill to think. She heard Fran's, Henry's, and Kurt's conversation as if it were coming from a tunnel. Her mind was so foggy from the drug, she could catch only a word here and there.

Finally she gave up trying and realized she felt as though she were floating. It wasn't an unpleasant feeling, so she simply surrendered, allowing herself to drift. The last thing she remembered before sleep was her vivid reliving the scene with Drake in the tower room.

She awakened to the memory of her fall. There was a dull thudding in her ankle, but it wasn't as swollen as it had been the night before. Fran had opened her draperies, and the bright sunlight streamed cheerfully into her bedroom. That stupid accident would certainly hamper her movements on this beautiful Sunday. The crutches beside her bed did nothing to improve her mood.

She scorned the crutches and hobbled from one piece of furniture to another toward the bath. Stepping into the shower, she turned it on, standing on her good foot while the water poured over her body in a refreshing torrent. After toweling her skin to dryness, she donned bright red lounging pajamas.

She was beginning to feel less like a zombie, but it wasn't easy to manage the bed steps.

Finally she was back in her bed and propped to a half-sitting position with pillows. At just the moment Holly realized she was hungry, Fran appeared with a breakfast tray of steaming hot coffee, scrambled eggs, hot biscuits, and strawberry preserves. Holly wasn't going to protest the calories, and she enjoyed every morsel of the food.

"Perhaps it would be better if you didn't try to tackle the stairs today," Fran said. "I can bring up your meals and whatever else you might need."

Holly thanked her warmly. By tomorrow she hoped she could manage the stairs, and without crutches.

When Fran left, she stretched luxuriously. It had been a long time since she'd spent an entire day lounging around, and she intended to make the best of it. It might even be fun.

Kurt called before noon, but she discouraged his driving out, saying she just wanted to rest and was feeling fine. Actually, she was studying her new weather-research book. Much she already knew, and parts of it were dull. Who really cared what United States city had the most sunshine? But there was quite a bit about weather phenomena from past years. She could weave a bit of that into weather-casts.

Holly pictured herself saying on her first weather-cast tomorrow: "When you're mopping your brow and feeling persecuted in our 105-degree temperature, just remember that during the ugly summer of 1936, your parents and grandparents were trying to deal with temperatures of 120 degrees. Doesn't that make you feel better?"

Holly put the book aside, leaned back against her pillows, and smiled with satisfaction. Her ankle was feeling so much easier that she was sure she would appear for work on Monday without the aid of crutches.

Pulling one pillow away from the others, she snuggled her face against it and closed her eyes. She must have slept, for the next thing she knew, it was late afternoon and Fran had tiptoed into her room with a pot of African violets and a note that said, "*Just to say once again that I'm sorry and I hope you're on the mend.*" It was signed with a large scrawly signature, "*Drake.*"

"It was really nice of him to go to so much trouble," Holly said to Fran, holding the note in her hand, carefully, as if it were fragile and valuable.

"Several people have called to ask how you're feeling, including Dr. Carlson," Fran said.

Holly expressed her appreciation, and when Fran had left her alone, she read the note at least a hundred times, as if it held some mysterious secret that she could uncover. She couldn't seem to keep her eyes away from the African violets, and much later, with the moonlight streaming into her bedroom, she drifted into sleep thinking that she would see Drake tomorrow.

8

~~~~~~~~~~~~~

Holly woke with the feeling that she had been on a long journey and now had reached her destination. Not even a sprained ankle was going to mar the joy of her first day as a television weathercaster. She didn't know how the ankle would feel when she put her weight on it, but other than twinges when she moved it around, there was no great pain.

Gingerly she removed the elastic wrap and discarded the sponge. There was still some swelling, and certainly the ankle was purplish and stiff, but she was sure she wouldn't need the crutches.

Carefully she replaced the elastic wrap before she got out of bed. She was gratified to find she could walk with only a slight limp and felt more soreness than pain.

She decided it would be a good idea to stay off her feet as much as possible before she went to work. But with prickles of anticipation constantly needling her, she found it impossible to read or even carve. Holly was glad that Fran was out running errands for most of the morning and wasn't around to tell her to take it easy. Every time her eyes strayed to the African violets that Drake had sent her, she felt an added burst of happiness.

Holly managed to make a project out of what to wear on her first day, mentally discarding first one garment and then the other. Finally she chose a traditional dirndl skirt of copper gabardine that was almost the exact color of her eyes, and with it a lighter, but blending, shirtwaist blouse. Certainly no one could fault her conservative attire.

But despite her stewing around, she was ready a full hour before it was time to arrive at the television station. Although it wasn't really necessary, since no bad weather was in the offing, she could go first to the Weather Bureau and check the weather charts. By the time she did that, it wouldn't be too early to arrive for work. With a last look at the African violets, and with proper deference to her injured ankle, Holly was on her way.

She had looked forward to thanking Drake for the violets, but it was the stocky news director, Hal Fitzgerald, who had been assigned to get her settled.

He greeted her warmly and said, "I'm glad your ankle is better. I heard about your accident, and Drake wasn't sure you'd be able to start today."

She refrained from saying that her fall hadn't been an accident, and she stifled her disappointment that Drake was nowhere in sight. Determinedly she turned her attention to Hal and followed him as he led the way down the hall. Halfway between the reception area and the control room, the news director stopped and opened the door to a small office.

"Here's where you'll hang your hat," he said.

She smiled, pleased that she wouldn't be working in a bull-pen atmosphere with typewriters clacking and newsmen milling in and out. And the office had a wide floor-to-ceiling window looking toward the mountains, with only a slightly different view from the one at her own bedroom window. Although she would have very little time to gaze out, it was comforting to know that the panoramic scene was there.

Holly went quickly to work preparing her first weathercast. She left her office door open and looked out into the hall every time anyone passed by. Surely Drake would come in and at least inquire about her ankle.

But it was Joyce Moore who all but pirouetted in, bubbling as usual, her dark blue eyes dancing. "Welcome aboard," she said. "Glad to see your ankle is better."

"Much, much better," Holly said.

Joyce looked at her wristwatch. "Did anyone tell you to check the videotape board when you come in each day? I think you're scheduled to do a commercial in a few minutes."

Holly thanked Joyce and followed her down the hall to the taping schedule just outside the studio door. Joyce was right. It was a commercial for an oil company, and she found the copy clipped to a board close by. Holly groaned. She was chagrined to see that the commercial was typed with Denise Warren's heading.

She forced her face into a smile, not wanting Joyce to know that she was slightly less than thrilled to be doing a commercial on her first day. She had so wanted the time to make her first weathercast outstanding!

Joyce patted Holly's shoulder, wished her good luck, and left Holly at her office door. She was startled to see a child's football jersey, including shoulder pads, a helmet, and a football, on her desk. Hurriedly scanning the copy for her commercial, she saw that she was expected to wear the offending apparel. The camera would shoot her from the waist up, so at least there were no football pants. The copy read: "Just as there are professionals in football, there are professionals in oil . . ." She felt the anger rise inside her.

Furiously she scooped up the football attire, including football, held the copy between her teeth, and limped down the hall toward the studio to find Bryan.

She found him with the videotape machines, editing a commercial. She waited for him to finish the edit he was working on, impatiently listening to the whir of the videotape as it wound back and forth for Bryan to find the exact spot for the edit. Then, unceremoniously, she dumped the gear in front of him.

"I won't do it," she sputtered. "I don't have the time, and I'm sure Drake doesn't intend for the station's weathercaster to appear in front of the camera looking ridiculous."

Bryan shrugged his lanky shoulders and cocked an eyebrow. "And on your first day," he said. "I really thought it would take longer for you to explode." He looked at her sympathetically. "I hate to tell you, but Drake will expect you to do whatever Denise

says. It's her account, and she brings in beaucoup
money to the station."

Holly fumed. She suspected that Denise Warren
brought a lot more than money to Drake. "Perhaps
the news director can stop this nonsense," she said
icily.

"I think you'll find that our news director takes his
orders from Drake."

Holly whirled around to find Denise speaking to
her coolly from the doorway. Holly froze.

Denise continued, "And I'm equally sure that you
had best get ready for the commercial." She looked
amused. "After your awkward fall, I really didn't expect you to be here at all."

Don't you wish, Holly said silently. It would take
more than being tripped on the dance floor and a
stupid commercial to get rid of her. There was nothing else to be done. She would simply have to do the
commercial.

She felt ridiculous in the football attire, and the
mirror verified the verdict that she looked absurd.
The football helmet was uncomfortable and the
shoulder pads kept slipping out of place.

Mercifully the thirty seconds was over, and wonder of wonders, Denise didn't ask that it be done
again. Holly's head was aching from the football
helmet, her ankle was throbbing, and her nose hurt
from the blow she received during rehearsal when
she had failed to catch the football and it hit her
nose instead.

What a miserable experience! And she was not to
be let off without a parting shot from Denise. "I
would advise you not to do any complaining to

Drake," she said haughtily, "and it will be to your advantage to stop making moon eyes at him. It simply won't do you any good."

So they were to have open warfare. Holly looked at Denise's smug face, and an impulse to slap it whipped through her, but she decided not to dignify the situation with any reply at all. She forced a smile in what she hoped was a "we'll-see" expression. At least it brought another warning from Denise: "Leave him alone or you'll be sorry."

Holly shrugged and turned her attention to the crew. They told her the commercial was fine, all except Nelson Sternum, who ran his hand through his shock of straw-colored hair and leered. Still no Drake. He surely must be away from the television station, but she didn't quite have the nerve to ask.

Holly looked at the studio clock and saw that she would have to rush to get ready for her weathercast. Her *first* weathercast, too! There would be no time to check again with the Weather Bureau.

She was anything but relaxed when at last the camera shifted to her for the weather report. Woodenly she gave her prepared comment on the 1936 hot weather, even stumbling over her words a couple of times. Inwardly fighting to overcome her nervousness, she had the opportunity during a commercial to breath deeply a number of times, and by the time she was on the air again for the local weather conditions, she was somewhat steadier. But when it was over, she knew that the weathercast had not been the greatest. Now she was glad that Drake wasn't around, and she prayed fervently that he hadn't been watching.

Leaving the television station for her supper break, she found Joyce filling in at the switchboard. "I was just awful," Holly wailed.

Joyce smiled comfortingly. "Not according to a couple of phone calls." She leaned toward Holly confidentially. "One man wanted to know all about that sweet thing who did the weather, and the other call came from a nice elderly woman who said you made the weather sound so pleasant."

The telephone rang again. Holly reflected that maybe she hadn't been as bad as she thought if at least two people had thought enough of her weathercast to call in. Anyway, she intended to do better at ten o'clock.

She listened to Joyce speaking on the telephone. "I'm sorry, we're not allowed to give out that information." When the conversation was over, Joyce turned to Holly with a troubled look. "Now, that's the kind of phone call we don't want," Joyce said. "Occasionally calls come in wanting an on-the-air person's home phone number and address. Mostly, they're kooks. This character wanted to tell you to stay at home and take care of your children."

Holly laughed. "That sounds harmless enough. Why didn't you tell him I would be happy to stay home with my children if I had any."

"He would have probably replied that you never would have any kids if you persisted in being a liberated woman," Joyce said. "But, seriously, you should get an unlisted telephone number. You can't tell when the calls are harmless or maybe dangerous." Joyce's dark blue eyes were serious. "Once in a while the calls are threatening. Anyway, you don't want to be bothered at home with a lot of calls."

"No worry there," Holly said. "My phone is listed in my grandmother's name."

"Gee, I almost forgot," Joyce said, slapping a hand across her forehead. "Drake called in on the mobile phone from his car and said that he would like to see you tomorrow."

Holly's heart jumped with excitement, but then she remembered her weathercast. "Oh, dear, he's probably displeased with my work already."

"No, he called while you were on the air, so he couldn't possibly have seen the weather segment."

Perversely, Holly thought Drake should have watched her first show, but it was good to know that he had thought about her. What could he want to talk with her about?

She was still pondering that question when she arrived at home for her supper break. Fran had really gone all out with a delicious spinach lasagna. Holly ate hungrily, recounting the afternoon's activities between bites of the tasty food. Fran sympathized with Holly's growing problem of Denise Warren.

"I do think that Drake Wimberly has more than a working interest in you, dear," Fran said seriously, but then laughed at her own pun.

Holly blushed and scolded herself for being pleased with Fran's remark. She would like to push all thoughts of Drake completely from her mind and concentrate on the work she had yearned to do. But it wasn't all that easy, with his leaving messages that he wanted to see her.

Back at the station after her supper break and

seated again behind her desk, she was presented with another message. Bryan appeared in his slow, "don't-rush-me" way. He said, "Joyce wanted you to know that another call came in after you left. A man said you should learn what you're doing, that you had better look at the sky before making fair-weather predictions."

Holly laughed, grateful that she had seen confirmation of her forecast, since she hadn't checked with the Weather Bureau before going on the air at six o'clock. "The clouds are fair-weather cumulus, Bryan," she explained. "They form in convective currents that are characterized by flat bases and dome-shaped tops. Fair-weather cumulus do not show extensive development and do not produce precipitation."

"You certainly sound learned." He laughed. "I'll leave the weather in your hands."

When Bryan left her office, she breathed a grateful prayer to her signposts in the sky and was really glad for the critical phone call. She could lead in to the weather tonight with an explanation of the fair-weather clouds.

With this decision, she felt at peace, and a new confidence took hold as she began her evening's work. When it was finally her turn for the weather during the late run, she felt as if she had been doing weathercasts forever. Indeed, within the "theater of her mind," this was true.

The entire crew congratulated her, except, once again, Nelson Sternum, who, hanging his headset on the camera, openly leered, as he had earlier. Apparently he was determined to be unpleasant, and she didn't know what to do about it.

Perhaps she would simply be nice and friendly toward him and he would eventually come around. She shrugged and soon forgot his rudeness in listening to the compliments. Particularly she appreciated Hal Fitzgerald's wink and pat on the back.

Holly was glowing by the time she reached home, but she was to hear more compliments from Fran. "And Henry said you looked like a veteran up there tonight," Fran said.

She kissed her grandmother on the cheek and thanked her. "It's been a long day," Holly said. Actually, she wasn't tired at all, only keyed up, but she wanted to be alone to savor her triumph. And surely fate wouldn't be so unkind as to keep Drake away from the television set when she had done so well.

She bade Fran a loving good night and went to her bedroom, singing a meaningless but happy ditty as she got ready for bed. She put on a cotton gauze nightgown of bright indigo blue, full and flowing. It fluttered at the sleeves and swirled about her feet, giving her a free-spirited feeling of wearing nothing but color. Opening the sliding glass doors to her gallery, she breathed deeply of the night air, sending thanks to the mountains and the universe for her good fortune.

Getting into bed, she realized that for hours, her ankle had given her nothing more than a twinge. Contentedly she wrapped her arms around the pillow as she usually did, and in that zone between waking and sleeping, she remembered with anticipation that Drake Wimberly wanted to see her to-morrow.

Holly arrived at the television station eagerly look-ing forward to seeing Drake. He was not going to be there all day. She would have to spend another restless night wondering why he wanted to see her.

9

On Wednesday Holly was awake with the first glow of morning. If sunsets in Oklahoma brought on a calm serenity, she decided, it was the pale pinks and vivid oranges of dawn that gave one the special aliveness, an "Okay, world, here I come!" feeling. By-passing the bed steps, she bounced from her bed to the floor, putting most of her weight on her left foot as a slight wince reminded her of her injury.

It was then that her eyes wandered to the basket of African violets and her heart gave an extra lilt. It would be hours before she could see him, so she might as well forget it for the moment. But her mind—or was it her heart?—kept returning to her en-counters with him, the kind of electric shock she'd felt when she first looked into his hazel eyes with their glinting brown and gold, that she had already learned could flip from teasing to tenderness to a superior look of coldness.

Sighing, she could almost feel his feather kiss on her lips. Their meeting in the tower room came to mind. How kind he had seemed in not wanting the baby birds in the chimney to be killed. Her arms were feeling again his fingers pressing into her flesh.

She rubbed her arm. Stop, she admonished herself, and vowed never again to think of Drake Wimberly in any way except as her employer.

While he might be willing to play a little game behind Denise Warren's back for heaven knows what reason, Holly certainly would not go along with it. From now on she would treat him with a chilly respect that was due one's employer.

To demonstrate her sincerity, she picked up the basket of violets and carted them downstairs to join a mass of Fran's plants in a corner of the kitchen. There, she said to herself, that should take care of that! And she intended to be a lot nicer to Kurt.

Just before leaving for work, she decided to call Kurt, feeling only a slight twinge of conscience when his voice sounded so eager. She readily agreed when he asked to pick her up for dinner.

"We'll go to Manuel's," Kurt said. "You haven't been there, have you?"

"No, but I hear the food is super, and you know how I love Mexican dishes."

Depositing the phone back in its cradle, she felt pleased with herself, and by the time she found herself waiting once again outside Drake Wimberly's office, she was thoroughly confident of her ability to cope with any attraction he had for her.

Holly's mirror and Fran's usual compliments had assured her that she looked very chic and charming in a soft suedecloth pantsuit of powder blue. Had it really been only five days ago that she had sat in this very chair almost on the verge of nervous prostration?

But her reaction to Drake when he emerged from his office and came toward her was no different from the first time. He was even handsomer than ever, dressed in white slacks and an exceptionally well-cut double-breasted blazer of dark blue with brass buttons.

Breathlessly she was aware of his look of approval when he saw her, and she managed only a slight twinge of weakness in her knees. He asked about her ankle, and when Holly assured him it was fine, he was all business.

"Let's talk in your office," he said, and his voice was almost formal, with none of the teasing in his eyes she had already grown to expect. Perhaps he sensed her determination to keep their relationship on a professional basis.

Neither spoke again until she was seated behind her desk and he stood before her, towered actually, his rangy body seeming to fill the room. Idly he walked over and fingered a book on her shelf, appearing perfectly at ease. But Holly was growing tense. He was certainly taking his time in getting around to saying whatever he had on his mind.

Finally he turned to her and spoke. "You were quite good on the ten-o'clock weather last night. Excellent, as a matter of fact."

Holly started to thank him, but was silenced by his cold stare. Obviously he had other things to say.

"The weather is just part of your job and remember you were warned about being a prima donna," he said. "I understand that you created quite a scene over doing the oil-company commercial."

Anger rose inside Holly. "Please, let me explain."

Drake interrupted her, his voice ominous. "There is nothing to explain. Such behavior will not be tolerated. I will expect your cooperation in the future."

Without giving her a chance to speak, he was gone. Holly gulped furiously, shutting her eyes tightly to hold back the tears. She had been right about Drake Wimberly in the first place!

He was arrogant, condescending, and impossible. She couldn't believe that Bryan had told him, so it must have been Denise who had wasted no time in getting to him.

He had certainly listened to her, but would not even give Holly a hearing. For a moment she was tempted to pick up her things and walk out, but through her anger, she knew that the job was too important. And wouldn't Denise just love her walking out? No, she would stay right here and show them all. Denise Warren was not going to get rid of her so easily.

Checking the videotaping schedule, she was thankful that she had only one simple commercial. Thank heaven it wasn't one of Denise's, just a straight announcer-on-camera message for an office-supply company.

She would have plenty of time to work on the weather. It was a good thing, because the weather was to be more of the same, hot with fair skies, westerly winds, and low humidity. She would be hard pressed for something interesting to say. Weathercasting on television became a real challenge when a replay of yesterday's show would do just as well.

Absorbed in her work, Holly was able to push the unpleasantness with Drake to the back of her mind, and by the time Kurt picked her up for dinner, she was her lively self again. Kurt certainly wasn't going to know that she was already having problems with her employer.

"I have a surprise for you," Kurt told Holly as they sped away from the television station. "Of course, I could easily stand a couple of hours alone with you, but I've invited Fran and Henry to join us. I know how much you enjoy them."

Holly was delighted and touched at Kurt's thoughtfulness. "How sweet of you," she said, reaching over to kiss him gently on the cheek. They rode along the boulevard, each giving out small bits of information about their activities. Holly carefully skirted her confrontation with Drake.

Suddenly Kurt stopped talking and Holly saw that he was looking intently into the rearview mirror.

"What is it?" she asked.

"The car behind us is really tailgating. If I had to stop in a hurry, it would crash into the back of us."

Holly turned around to look, but the car had slowed its speed and was falling behind. It was a green late model, but it could have been any make.

She wasn't all that good at telling the difference in the various automobiles.

"We got rid of him anyway," she said, relaxing again in her seat.

The incident was all but forgotten by the time they reached Manuel's. Fran and Henry were already seated at a table. Holly was amused that although the table would easily seat six people, they were sitting side by side, talking animatedly as if they could never catch up with each other's news. Holly felt a twinge of envy, but quickly rebuked herself.

She looked around the restaurant at the decor, loving the Mexican atmosphere. All stucco and tile, blue and white tile intermingled with baskets of artificial flowers and fruit hanging about. There were several fireplaces that must make the restaurant a cozy place in winter.

Then, along with the others, Holly turned her attention to the menu. The decision was easy. It was the house special for all of them. Manuel's special enchiladas, tamales, chili con queso, rice, beans, and tacos had all the earmarks of a real feast. The bottle of Chianti in its colorful straw basket arrived and the waiter with an elaborate flourish filled the wineglasses.

Fran raised her glass in a toast. "To our future, whatever it might hold."

Holly joined the other three in the toast, but took only a sip of the wine. She didn't want her senses dulled, because her day's work wasn't over until after the ten-o'clock weather.

The restaurant was filling up rapidly for the dinner

hour and she judged that soon not a single table
would be available. She saw Kurt looking around,
too, when suddenly he pushed his chair away from
the table and stood up. "Excuse me for a moment,"
he said.

Before Holly could speculate on Kurt's abrupt departure, Fran spoke. "Sorry I missed your telecast at
six," she said. "How did it go?"

"Very well," Holly answered, and it had gone well
in spite of her reprimand from Drake, a reprimand
that she wasn't likely to forget. Now she wished he
would hurry and find a new manager so that she
would never have to see him again. In the meantime, she would stay out of his way as much as possible.

Knocked out of ten years' growth! Grand Ben's favorite phrase whenever he was startled or surprised
flitted through her mind when she saw why Kurt
had left the table. He had returned with Denise and
Drake in tow.

"I spotted them waiting for a table and asked
them to join us," Kurt explained proudly.

Oh, Kurt, if you only knew. Holly spoke to him
silently.

She simply could not meet Drake's eyes for fear
he would see the contempt she felt and fire her on
the spot. As for Denise, she really had a nerve. Certainly Drake Wimberly and Denise Warren were the
last two people in the world she wanted to see. How
nice, Holly thought bitterly, since they both had the
same initials, Denise wouldn't even have to change
her monogram when they got married.

Apparently Holly was the only one who wasn't

delighted with the arrangement. Denise obviously had decided to be "Miss Congeniality." Seated next to Fran, Denise began to question Fran enthusiastically about her doll collection.

"I've heard that it's simply fabulous," Denise said. "In fact, after we order our food, I'd like to talk to you and Kurt about an idea I have."

It was unbelievable to Holly that Drake acted as if nothing at all had happened between them, that he hadn't accused her of being a prima donna and causing a scene. He even patted her arm as he took the chair beside her, and leaned forward to talk with Henry.

"I've been checking out that wind-power-generator location," Drake said to Henry. So that was why Holly hadn't seen Drake on her first days at work. If he had been there, she thought resentfully, maybe he would have understood. Drake continued, "It looks all right to me. What made you pick that particular spot?"

"Wind-speed measurements over low, smooth hills give surprisingly higher readings than the surrounding plains," Henry said. "That location has lots of trees that have been deformed by the wind, so it should be an excellent wind-power site."

"Isn't that amazing?" Drake spoke to Holly as if nothing was wrong between them.

She couldn't even bring herself to smile, but was saved from any embarrassment by the waiter's bringing their food order and waiting for Denise and Drake to look at the menu and place their order.

Wineglasses were brought for Denise and Drake,

and everyone's glass was filled again, except Holly's, which was still nearly full. Her food remained practically untouched, too. Each mouthful felt as if it would choke her.

After the waiter had gone, Denise demanded everyone's attention. "I have the greatest idea for an insurance commercial," she said, smiling coyly at Kurt and then turning to Fran. "If you could lend me a few of your dolls and a dollhouse, I'd like to put the commercial together, and then, if Kurt likes it, we would place a schedule on Channel 33. It really would be good for your business, Kurt."

Fran agreed that Denise could borrow the dolls and dollhouse, and Kurt said, "I can't imagine an insurance commercial like that, but I'll keep an open mind."

"That's all I ask," Denise said. "You won't be committing yourself until you see and like what we've done."

"Sounds mysterious, but I'm game." Kurt smiled at Denise.

Fran spoke. "Why don't all three of you come to dinner tomorrow night, and Denise can see the dolls and decide which she wants to use."

Good grief, was it never going to end, this constant association with Denise and Drake? Holly was appalled, but hoped they would refuse.

No such luck. It was only Kurt who couldn't be there because of a meeting. Drake said, "Holly won't have to leave after dinner, because our ten-o'clock newscast will be preempted by a network special tomorrow night."

Oh, joy, thought Holly in disgust. Maybe she

could find some excuse to leave, or maybe not be there at all. But at least she could get away from them now. Glancing at her watch, she saw that it was time for her to get back to work. Fran and Henry stayed to visit with Denise and Drake.

Immediately upon her return to the station, she checked with the Weather Bureau. The five-day forecast had changed, and it appeared that by the weekend there might be a break in the hot weather. There could be a few rain showers.

She had just replaced the phone when Bryan came in her office. "You've had another phone call from your admirer," he said slowly, "the one who wants you to stay home and have kids."

Holly smiled at Bryan. "What this time?" she asked curiously.

Bryan's frown creased his forehead. "I doubt that it's anything to be concerned about, but he did say he would find a way to get you off the tube and that he hoped violent measures wouldn't be necessary."

"I'm not worried," she said. "He probably has nothing better to do than make telephone calls. Did he sound young or old?"

"Hard to tell. His voice is heavily accented."

Holly waved a hand in the air. "In the meantime, we may have a weather change. Maybe if I can bring our mystery man some rain and cooler weather, he'll simmer down."

By the time her weathercast was over, she was once again feeling the satisfaction from her work. Pulling into her home driveway, she was singing the song, "There'll Be Some Changes Made." Denise Warren and Drake Wimberly could throw up all the barriers they liked. "The horrid two DW's," as she decided to dub them, would not drive her away from the job she loved.

"My, aren't you in a delightful mood?" Fran said. "You looked so out-of-sorts at dinner." Fran was sitting on the couch, sewing a rip in the seam of a doll dress and listening to television. She got up and turned off the set. "You were super tonight. Thanks for giving us hope for some rain."

"Glad to oblige," Holly answered gaily, flopping into Grand Ben's old chair and kicking off her shoes. "However, the weather change is only a chance, not a certainty."

They talked until Holly noticed that Fran was beginning to look sleepy-eyed. Glancing at her watch, Holly was out of the chair and on her feet, picking up her shoes without putting them on.

"Almost midnight, and I'm off to dreamland," she said.

But once in bed, her mind kept jumping from one subject to another, returning with monotonous frequency to Drake Wimberly and the way he had hurt her. She would not allow her thoughts to dwell there. She had closed the book on that one, and no longer would she allow him to affect her in any way. Still, her last thoughts before drifting into sleep were of Drake.

She awoke with the memory of his hand touching her arm. With a sigh she despaired of ever getting him out of her mind.

It was early, and even if she had gone to bed at such a late hour, she was wide-awake, trying to decide what to do with the hours that stretched in front of her before she could go to work.

She remembered what was facing her tonight, wondered how she'd ever get through the evening with Denise and Drake on hand.

How Fran could have invited them, Holly couldn't imagine, except that she loved to cook for company. Thankfully Henry would be here, so she could concentrate on him and Fran as much as possible. With that decided, Holly settled down after breakfast on her gallery to finish the last of the carving on the weather vane.

10

"It's perfect," she concluded, looking at the miniature weathercock before leaving for work. On an impulse, she took it with her. Perhaps she could think of a way to use it on her show.

By the time she was seated at her desk, Holly had decided to hold up the small object at the opening of the weather and say something like, "Reddy Weathercock says, 'A gentle breeze is blowing southerly a soft seven to ten miles an hour.' And the Weather Bureau and I say that tomorrow brings a

sixty percent chance for rain showers, some likely
heavy."

As she looked out her window toward the mountains and the gathering clouds, it seemed doubtful
that the moisture would hold off more than a few
hours. The sky reminded her of a quote she had
read somewhere. The clouds "looked as though an
angel in his upward flight had left his mantle
floating in midair."

"Studying the weather?" a now familiar voice
quipped in her ear.

She turned slowly, wanting to compose her expression before she faced Drake Wimberly. She intended to appear cool and businesslike, so she
looked at him without replying. He needn't think
she had forgiven him for unfairly reprimanding her,
but inside she was quivering and breathless.

"You're certainly the original Miss Solemn Face,"
he said amiably. How easily he switched the heavy
boss act on and off.

"I was simply trying to decide if it was going to
rain tonight," she answered stiffly.

"You look as if to rain or not to rain is your decision."

Holly steeled herself to keep from responding to
his bantering mood with something like: How do
you know it's not my decision? Instead, she picked
up the weathercock and suggested that she'd like to
open the weathercast with it.

"Why not?" he said. "There's an electric fan back
in the prop room. I'll get Bryan to set it up to see if
the fan will move it. Okay?"

Darn, it wasn't easy to keep her bad humor with

him. He could be so nice. "Thank you," she said, and couldn't help smiling into his eyes that were looking at her so winningly.

He laughed, a heartwarming sound that made her heart leap. He took the weathercock from her and leaned across her desk to kiss the tip of her nose. "Now, that's better," he said. "I'll see you at dinner tonight."

Yes, and you'll be with Denise, she said silently. When he was gone, she reminded herself that anything special was between him and that woman, not with her. But despite the warning to herself, she touched the tip of her nose. She did feel much better.

By six o'clock she didn't need for the Weather Bureau to tell her that within the hour Arrowhead would get its first good soaking in three months. The rain had already obscured her view of the mountains, and it was moving in.

The show went well, and Reddy Weathercock behaved nicely before the electric fan. Outside, the wind had picked up a bit before the coming rain. Then, just as she was leaving the studio, she heard a loud Donald Duck quacking beside her.

She turned to see Nelson Sternum. "Gonna be a ducky night, a night for werewolves and goblins that eat little weather girls," he said, running his hand through his shock of straw-colored hair, free now of it encumbering headset.

Holly thought he was only being friendly, when she noted the contemptuous, almost sinister look in his eyes. She shivered. Apparently he was never going to forgive her for her slight on that first day.

Nonetheless, she smiled shakily at him before heading down the hall.

Since she wouldn't be coming back tonight, she took a few minutes to straighten up her desk and office. She even decided to dust the top of her desk. She finished and was headed out the station door when she remembered that the weathercock was still in the studio. Impatiently she retraced her steps, but Reddy had disappeared. Bryan and Joyce, who was waiting for him, helped her search for the weathercock, but it was futile. Who on earth could have taken it?

"Maybe it will turn up later," Bryan said. Holly apologized for holding them up and decided to check her office to see if someone had put the weathercock on her desk.

At the office door, her eyes widened and she gasped at the sight on her desk. The weathercock lay there, sprayed with red paint. She sighed, thinking of the hours she had lovingly spent turning an ordinary piece of wood into the weathercock. Who would have done such a thing?

She walked over to her desk and saw the note beside it, the weathercock lying on the notepaper. At least the person had been kind enough not to get the paint on her desk.

Just see what can happen to little weather forecasters, the note said. Surely the words didn't mean to threaten her, but what else could they mean? She must have an enemy already among the studio crew. Only Nelson and Denise had shown any animosity toward her, but despite his jabs, she didn't really think Nelson would do it. And Denise hadn't been there at all.

It was good that she wouldn't have to return to the station tonight. She leaned against the door for a moment to stop shaking, and she was glad for the first time that Fran had invited Drake to dinner, even with Denise. He might have some inkling of who was responsible.

A few sprinkles were coming down as she drove away, and it began to rain hard before she reached the turnoff toward home. If it wasn't raining, she wouldn't need headlights, but the blue-black sky had caused early darkness. Just as she switched on her lights, a car behind her did the same.

She hadn't noticed the car before, and she remembered the tailgating experience with Kurt the previous night. No reason to be afraid, she told herself. But she did admit to nervousness from her recent experience. Perhaps it would be best to lock the car doors. She was relieved when, turning into the winding lane toward home, the other car continued on down the road.

With the rain and the growing darkness, she couldn't determine the color of the car. It was ridiculous even for a moment to think that the car had been following her. She didn't intend to mention it to anyone at dinner.

Holly spotted Henry's Chrysler beside Drake's four-wheeler. Parked just on the other side was a small Fiat convertible she knew must belong to Denise. She couldn't help but be pleased that the two of them hadn't come together. Pulling out her umbrella from the backseat, she raised it and raced for the house, puddles of water soaking her shoes and splattering her hose. The driving rain drenched her suit, too.

Despite her wetness, she was relaxed and in control of herself when she was inside and had greeted the foursome amid choruses from Henry, Fran, and Drake that her weathercast had been tremendous. She noticed that Denise said nothing, only looked bored with the attention Holly was receiving. It was hard not to laugh at Drake, who was puffed up with pleasure that the opening with Reddy Weathercock had worked so well.

She wanted to change out of her wet garments immediately. Later, she could tell them what had happened with Reddy Weathercock.

"We were just about to send a search party after you," Fran said when Holly rejoined them, comfortably clad in a panther print tunic over black pants. In looks, she realized she was no match for Denise, who was wearing a shocking-pink sundress with one white embroidered daisy on the skirt. But when her eyes turned to Drake, he looked at her as if she had a certain charm.

"With that panther and jungle on the front of you, we can open the next weathercast on just your midriff. It will make a fetching picture," he joked.

She laughed, but sobered when telling about the red paint being sprayed on the weathercock.

Drake was as mystified as she had been. He spoke grimly. "We'll get to the bottom of this, Holly," he said. "I'll call a meeting of the entire production crew tomorrow. While I'm sure it was meant only as a prank by someone who didn't realize Reddy's value in carving hours, nonetheless, the person responsible will be fired."

Holly fervently hoped that it was meant only as a prank. "I would feel bad to see anyone fired," she said.

"I simply will not tolerate such things." He spoke with such vehemence that she knew it was useless to argue.

"I can sand and varnish it," Henry said. "I'm sure it will look just fine."

"That's settled, then," Denise said brightly, and turned to Holly. "We were having such an interesting conversation when you came in. Drake and Henry were talking about building the wind-power generator. Simply fascinating." Her tone implied that Holly was intruding. Sitting beside Drake on the couch, she tucked her arm through his possessively. Holly doubted that Denise was all that interested in wind power. She just wanted to impress Drake.

"I think that subject was about exhausted," Drake said, but although his eyes were on Holly, he patted Denise's arm as if appreciating her interest.

Dinner was Fran's usual culinary success. A delicious casserole of chili grits, fruit salad, a green salad, and corn on the cob. Everyone ate with gusto. Even Holly couldn't seem to get enough to eat. And from the way Drake devoured the pecan pie, Holly was sure he could have eaten half the pie.

Denise was very pleasant to her, even enthusiastically so, when she talked about the commercials she would write for Holly to do the announcing. "With your drama training, there are so many possibilities," Denise concluded.

Why, when Denise was so complimentary, did Holly feel such a sense of foreboding? If Denise had been at the television station, she would have been sure that Denise had sprayed the red paint on the weathercock.

Denise continued to monopolize the conversation when the party adjourned to the den for coffee. She told them about the commercials that were planned for a furniture store, putting the furniture in a natural setting in the Wichita Mountains. "It has simply taken forever to get the permits to shoot for commercial purposes in the wildlife refuge." Then she turned to Holly and spoke sweetly. "I do wish you had been here earlier, but we have another announcer scheduled. Anyway, Saturday is your day off, isn't it?"

Even on her day off, Holly would have enjoyed the trip to the mountains, and doing those commercials would be fun. She looked down so that Denise couldn't see her disgruntled expression.

Holly was sure that Denise was interested in Holly's doing only commercials that made her look stupid. She knew that, because of Kurt, Denise would have Holly do the commercial using the doll and dollhouses. She just hoped sho wouldn't have to wear a doll dress, complete with doll's cap.

As if picking up her thoughts, Fran turned to Denise. "Shall we walk over to Doll Heaven so that you can decide on the dolls and house you would like to use?"

Outside, the rain had stopped, and clouds drifted

in gossamer wisps over the full moon. Holly, trailing the others, stopped for a moment to enjoy the coolness and sweet rain-washed air. Drake dropped back, too, and took both of Holly's hands in his. "Don't worry, little one, I'll see that you have no more trouble with anyone at the station."

His voice was so husky, so tender, that she couldn't believe that this was the same man who had spoken to her so roughly about doing commercials. A warmth was melting her inside, and she would have liked nothing more than to lean against his strong body, but it was neither the time nor the place.

There never will be a time or a place, Holly thought sadly. Denise will see to that. Later, she would work again on her resolve to have only a working relationship with him. And she was certain that Drake didn't mean Denise when he said she'd have no more trouble. Drake took her arm and guided her toward the log cabin.

Denise gave Drake a sharp look when he and Holly joined the others already inside. But Denise's attention was soon drawn to the dolls and dollhouses. She chose Holly's favorite dollhouse, with its ranch-style look and eclectic decor. The dolls she wanted to use were of the family of Ginny dolls and the Jumeau doll.

"I'm very excited about this commercial, and I know Kurt will love it," Denise said. "The opening calls for a close-up of a man's face, a man with lots of strength in his countenance." She looked at Drake coyly. "And Drake has finally agreed to do it."

"But not willingly," Drake replied, laughing.

Holly's heart sank when Drake looked at Denise as if he could refuse her nothing.

"If he hadn't agreed, I might have persuaded Henry to take the part," Fran said, gazing with tender eyes at her man, whose face was lined with character and strength.

Sweethearts on parade, Holly thought, feeling suddenly like the proverbial fifth wheel. It was too bad Kurt couldn't be here. She could have at least put on an act of really being smitten with him. For shame, Holly, she said to herself. That wouldn't be fair to Kurt.

The loneliness that gripped her stayed the remainder of the evening, and she still had that lost, out-of-tune feeling when Drake, Denise, and Henry had gone.

She asked Fran to wake her early, slowly walked up the stairs to her bedroom, and mechanically prepared to retire for the night. The unfamiliar ache inside her was so strong that she expected to stay awake. But she was thankful that her ankle had given her practically no trouble today. Maybe by tomorrow she wouldn't even know she'd ever had a sprained ankle.

Holly punched at her pillow as if it were responsible for her sleeplessness. Finally she must have slept, for the next thing she knew, Fran was in her bedroom with a steaming cup of hot coffee.

It must be morning, and she remembered that Drake was going to call a meeting to try to find the person who had sprayed the red paint on her weather vane.

11

~~~~~~~~~~~~

Joyce Moore, her eyes wide and as darkly blue today as a midnight sky, was waiting for Holly when
she arrived at work. "Drake has been a madman,"
Joyce said excitedly. "He's raked this television station from one end to the other and quizzed everyone
who was here last evening when your weathercock
was sprayed with paint."

"Surely not you?" Holly said.

"Me, too," Joyce replied ruefully, "when everyone
knows I'm a menace with a spray can of any description. Hair spray goes on the mirror instead of
my hair. And the last time I tried to clean the
bathroom, I got a face full of foam. I can never seem
to get the nozzle pointed in the proper direction."

Holly laughed uproariously at Joyce's narrative of
her shortcoming.

"From the way Drake's acting, I'd swear he is
more than paternally interested in you," Joyce
added.

Holly's heart leaped, but she said demurely, "I'm
sure he's simply appalled at any vandalism taking
place here."

Joyce shook her head decidedly. "I've never seen

him act this way. He said that the incident won't be forgotten and whoever did it had better watch his step."

"I'd hate for anyone to think I was demanding that the culprit be punished," Holly said thoughtfully.

Bryan's voice over the intercom asked Holly to report to the studio. Holly looked questioningly at Joyce.

"The doll commercial," Joyce said.

"I didn't even know the dolls had been picked up," Holly said in surprise. "I must have been dressing for work."

"They're here." Joyce smiled. "The dolls and house are adorable."

By the time Holly reached the studio, she saw that everything was almost ready for the commercial. Denise was coaching Drake, trying to get the right expression on his face. He looked so uncomfortable, Holly had to laugh. Certainly he was no limelighter. As Denise tried to show him how she wanted him to look into the camera, he contorted his face into various horrible grimaces. Even she chuckled when he tried to imitate the Hunchback of Notre Dame.

He waved to Holly and she smiled in return, feeling the warmth and intimacy of people working well together on a project. That really was the key, wasn't it? If she could maintain an offhand friendliness toward Drake, all would be well.

Picking up her copy, she took her place on the high stool and clipped the small chest mike in place. Her eyes went over the opening lines, rehearsing them silently: "Every man has his private world. It begins with his family and his love for them." The camera would open on Drake's face looking toward the spot where the Jumeau doll would be edited in at the upper right of the television screen. The doll would be in a circle cutout.

The other camera then switched to a shot of the dollhouse as Holly said, "It grows with possessions of property and investments. But private worlds are subject to sudden crumbling." There the fan blew over the Ginny dolls.

At that point, a hand stood up one of the Ginnys as the camera zoomed in for a close-up, and Holly said, "Yet many of them are able to rise again from disaster." It was here that the camera would come to Holly on screen to give the insurance pitch. The commercial ended with the camera once again on the dollhouse and Holly's suggesting that everyone should protect his private world with Kurt's insurance.

Grudgingly she admitted that Denise had written a good commercial. Kurt was sure to like it when it was finished. Everyone pronounced it superb, and Denise had no criticism of Holly's part.

It was the one commercial Holly had really enjoyed doing, but nonetheless she was glad to get her mind back on her first love, the weather. She was putting the temperatures around the nation on the weatherboard when Drake came into the studio.

"I've made no headway toward solving the weathercock mystery, but I'm not giving up," he assured her.

"I'm somewhat embarrassed," she said. "I don't

want to get the reputation for continually causing a problem."

"I can understand that." Drake's face darkened. "But in this case, it wasn't you who caused the problem."

Holly could have bitten off her tongue for blatantly reminding him that she had caused a scene over the football commercial. But before Holly could reply, Joyce hurried into the studio.

"You have a visitor," she told Drake grimly. "Jim Carstairs."

Holly remembered Jim Carstairs was the manager Drake had fired.

"I can't believe he'd show his face again in this television station." Drake's voice was cold and forbidding. "Or that he'd have the nerve to want to see me."

"He's very quiet and subdued," Joyce said. "He asked almost humbly if you could spare a few minutes."

Drake sighed, running his hand through his dark hair. He turned to Holly. "I'd better get this over with."

Joyce lingered to speculate with Holly on the former television manager's appearance.

"I can't imagine that Drake would see him," Holly said.

"Drake's a very compassionate man," Joyce replied. "Once a conflict is over, he never gives it another thought. Once I didn't catch two automobile dealers' commercials running one after the other. That's okay in newspapers, but not on television. Drake was furious, but couldn't remember what I was talking about when I brought it up several days later."

Holly smiled and posted the last temperature on the weatherboard. Ninety-four degrees in Houston.

"With Houston's humidity, that's like a hundred and ten degrees here," Joyce commented as they both turned to leave the studio.

"Traffic on the freeways is enough to cope with," Holly said, "and I hear that several thousand people move to Houston every week."

"I understand some Houstonians have a new saying, 'Yankee go home.'" Joyce paused at Holly's office doorway to conclude the conversation.

Holly chuckled. "I must remember to tell that to Henry Olsen. He's a born-again rebel and still fighting the Civil War."

Joyce laughed, walking on to her own office.

Alone, Holly turned her thoughts to Joyce's remarks about Drake's quickly forgetting his anger. Would he also forget that she'd caused a turmoil over the football commercial? Fervently she hoped so, and vowed that no matter what happened, she would be one hundred percent cooperative and even-tempered.

A pleasant tingling started in her solar plexus and moved swiftly to her heart. He did seem to have a human, lovable side.

Lovable? She leaned back in her desk chair, shut her eyes, and examined the feelings that were going on inside her body. A sudden stabbing sweetness, almost like pain, thrilled through her, leaving her breathless. Was it possible that she was in love with him?

No, that mustn't happen. He was her employer and obviously involved with Denise. Holly reminded herself that she was enough like Fran that she couldn't bear to be dominated.

Wasn't it evident that Drake would control every person, place, and thing in his orbit? But her logical arguments didn't take away the bubbling excitement.

The afternoon had simply sped away. Heading once again for the studio, she clipped on her mike and waved to Hal Fitzgerald, who was ready to do his newscast. She paid little attention to the news, involved with her own thoughts, so involved that she was almost taken by surprise when it was her turn for the weather. But she had no trouble smiling all the way through the weathercast.

"You really sparkled through that one," Bryan told her afterward.

"It's easy to smile today," she answered, but with no explanation. She was in love with the entire world, and Drake Wimberly had nothing to do with it.

Drake came into the studio just as she was leaving. "Good show," he said, but was obviously distracted, his face strained. "That was very painful," he said, jerking a thumb in the direction of his office. "Jim Carstairs literally begged for his job back." Drake scowled. "I really wish I could give it to him, but that's impossible."

Holly realized that he did have a lot of compassion for people. Joyce joined them and said to Holly, "Your friend called again. He insists that you're destined for motherhood and twelve kids."

"I'd hate to lose a good weathercaster," Drake joked, "but I guess I couldn't interfere with such a worthy cause."

Holly blushed and started to say that she was far from ready for that step, but Drake grew serious. "How often does he call?"

"Almost every day," Joyce replied. "He said he must get her off the tube."

Drake brooded. "I'm not sure the word 'tube' is used widely outside the industry. I wonder if it could be the same person who sprayed the weathercock red?"

Holly remained silent, but she certainly wasn't alarmed, not with all the effervescent sensations going on inside. She devoutly hoped Drake couldn't guess the effect he had on her.

Joyce spoke. "His voice sounds staged. He had a heavy accent, which may not be his real voice at all."

"Then it could easily be someone inside the station," Drake said, and turned to Holly. "If you're ready to leave, I'll walk with you." They went out to her Sunbird. "When you return tonight, lock your car and park directly by the door," he commanded. "I'll tell Bryan to watch for you. We don't want to take any chances."

Holly started to protest until she saw the concern on his face. A quiver ran along her spine. Could she possibly mean more to him than just an employee? Certainly not, she scolded herself. He'd show the same interest in anyone.

"Tell Fran we'll get the dolls and house back in

the next hour or so," he said as he helped her into the car. "Be careful."

"Thank you," she said, and smiled, hoping her face didn't reveal the way her pulse was bouncing. Her heart sang as she sped home, and she was almost glad for the telephone calls. Even if he would be equally concerned about anyone else, she was secretly glad he was making a fuss over her. She felt sure that the calls were only crank ones and the sprayed paint on the weathercock had been a harmless prank.

Henry's car was parked in its usual spot. Upon entering the house, she could hear their ridiculous argument. She shook her head and smiled ruefully.

Henry was saying, "If the South had won, our southern ways would have been preserved and our women would still be protected."

"In that case, I'm mighty glad they lost," Fran retorted. "You know, Henry, I'm no hothouse flower to be swaddled in crinoline and old lace."

Dressed in jeans and a bright plaid shirt, Fran certainly backed up her words. Holly laughed. "You two are impossible," she said. "Can't you just see Fran in hoop skirts and scads of petticoats?"

"It was all those clothes as much as anything else that kept women tied down," Fran said. "Once we were free of those endless yards of material, we could move around and take our rightful place."

Holly laughed again at Fran's logic, but Henry was still on the verge of seriousness. "She'd be beautiful in a ball gown. Make no mistake about that," he said stubbornly.

After a few more exchanges, Henry ended his

visit, declining Fran's and Holly's joint supper invitation. After he had gone, the two women decided to eat in the den on TV trays, enjoying a light supper of chicken salad, an avocado, and big glasses of lemonade.

"Delicious," Holly pronounced, moving her empty plate to one side and stretching her arms above her head. "It's so good to relax."

"It is, isn't it?" Fran grinned. "Henry can be really trying with his insistence that the South could have won the war."

"Can't you see he's just needling you? It's a harmless enough fixation, and it gives you both an outlet for any of life's frustrations. Why don't you give up and marry him?"

"I don't see you running to the altar with Kurt," Fran said with a toss of her head.

"But I'm not in love with Kurt," Holly replied. "And you're obviously in love with Henry."

Fran gave a wide cheery smile. "Shows that much, does it? I thought I was hiding it pretty well."

"Not from me, and I doubt from Henry."

Suddenly a loud knock on the door interrupted their conversation. They looked questioningly at one another. Who could it be?

12

ᘛᘛᘛᘛᘛᘛᘛᘛᘛᘛ

"It must be your dolls and dollhouse," Holly said, getting up from the couch. When she switched on the porch light and opened the door expecting to greet one of the floor crew, she was startled to be face to face with Drake. His countenance was stern and unsmiling.

"If we can have the key to the log cabin," he said, "we'll unload." Fran, directly behind her, handed Drake the key to Doll Heaven.

Drake took the key and looked gravely at both of them. He hesitated before speaking again. Finally he said formally, "After we've unloaded, I must talk with you."

Fran and Holly looked at him questioningly and said in unison, "Of course. But what—"

He held up his hand. "It will take only a few minutes to unload, then I'll be back."

They stared at his rapidly retreating back, shut the door, and returned to the den to speculate on Drake's strange behavior.

"Was he talking to both of us, or just you?" Fran asked.

"No way to tell," Holly said, but she was remembering that he acted the same way when he had reprimanded her about the football commercial.

What could she possibly have done now? Coldness grew inside her, and her knees were shaking. The doll commercial had gone well, and of course, there had been that silly phone call.

Was it possible that she had done something so terrible that he was going to fire her? But wouldn't he have waited until she was at work?

She walked around the room, absently touching one object after another, and occasionally wiping away imaginary dust. It was not possible to relax until she knew what had caused his tight-lipped sternness. Apparently Fran felt the same way, but she busied herself with making coffee.

The coffee was ready when Drake knocked once again. When Fran handed him a cup of coffee, he said, "I really need this, thank you." But he certainly didn't look as if a cup of coffee would fix whatever was wrong with him.

Holly motioned him toward Grand Ben's easy chair, while she and Fran took places on the couch. Drake had certainly communicated his mood to both of the women. The vibrations in the room were tense and foreboding.

"I really don't know how to tell you this," Drake said stiffly, looking at Fran.

"Then perhaps you'd better just say it," Fran suggested gently.

He took a deep breath. "The big doll has been stolen," he said. "Someone took it from the prop room between the time we finished the commercial and the time we moved the wagon around to the back to load up."

"I can't believe it!" Fran cried.

Holly was stunned. The new Jumeau doll!

"I know the doll is valuable," Drake said. "I've called the police, and of course the station's insurance will take care of the monetary loss if the doll isn't recovered. I'm so sorry."

"It isn't your fault," Fran said, but she looked distressed.

"I'm responsible. Nothing like this has ever happened before." He paused to sip his coffee. "We constantly have thousands of dollars in merchandise at the studio. Even small things like diamond rings that could easily be taken."

"I'm sure the police will find the doll," Fran said, cheering.

"Maybe I'm a jinx." Holly really felt like one at the moment.

Drake didn't bother to deny her statement. "The back door was locked, so the doll had to have been carried through the studio and out the front door. I just don't see how that was possible."

"Perhaps it was someone who had a key to the prop-room door," Holly said.

"The key hangs by the door, so it could have been done that way." Drake frowned. "Simply unlock the door until the thief could come around to the back and take the doll."

"Then come back in, lock the door, and go out through the front," Holly finished.

"That's a lot of moving around not to be noticed," he said.

The three of them were silent, digesting the speculations. Suddenly something about the way Drake sat in the chair, as if he meant to sit there forever, made Holly sense that there was more to the story.

"Is there something you haven't told us?" she asked quietly.

Drake looked at her, amazement showing on his face. "The theft is bad enough," he said, and hesitated, "but, yes, there is more."

Fran and Holly watched him tensely.

Drake sat his coffee cup on the table beside the chair and reached in his pocket, pulling out a piece of paper. "I don't want to frighten you, and I debated about telling you at all," he said, "but I'm sure it's better if you know and we take precautions."

"Precautions?" Holly asked.

He handed Holly the piece of paper with big block printing, just like the weather-vane note. Holly read the words aloud: "*I've already shown you what can happen to little weathercasters. Next time it could be the real live doll.*" She handed the note back to Drake and shuddered. "The note's talking about me." She couldn't help the catch in her voice. "First the weathercock, and now the doll."

"I came out with the boys in the station wagon, so I can ride back to the station with you. I'll wait until the newscast is over and follow you home."

Holly was grateful for the offer, but said, "I hate to be all that much trouble. Do you really think it's necessary for you to wait?"

"Yes, I do," he replied firmly. In spite of the seriousness of the situation, a delicious shiver moved up her spine at the prospect of being with him most of the evening. He continued, "I thought about taking you off the ten-o'clock weathercast until this is all over and—"

"Oh, no!"

He looked at her sympathetically. "We do need you on the late run," he said. "And, of course, you'll be away from the television station over the weekend. If it's not settled by Monday, I'll arrange for a police car to follow you."

"Do you really think it's that dangerous?"

"Maybe it will all be over and we won't need to do that." He glanced at his watch. "Right now we'd better get you to work."

Holly left the den to freshen her makeup, and minutes later she handed Drake the keys to her Sunbird for him to drive. She had to laugh when he struggled to get his long legs into the small car.

Sitting next to him on the way to the television station, she enjoyed prickles of excitement which had nothing to do with any danger to her. She was content to sit quietly while Drake speculated on the theft of Fran's prized doll, commenting only occasionally.

Drake said, "I can't get away from the fact that Jim Carstairs was there, and perhaps could have been there when the weathercock was sprayed with the paint." He paused. "On the other hand, I don't see how he could have been around and no one be aware of it."

"Do you suppose he might still have keys to the doors?" Holly asked.

"That's possible," Drake said thoughtfully.

"And if Jim Carstairs did have a key to the prop room," Holly said, "it wouldn't have been too difficult for him to hide there and wait for his chance to spray paint on the weathercock."

"But I can't see how he could possibly have gotten to your office without being seen," Drake said.

When they reached the television station, Drake went directly to his office and Holly to her office to call the Weather Bureau and get ready for the weathercast. She found it difficult to concentrate with this mystery in the air. She had just reached for the telephone when Drake interrupted her.

"The police have interrogated Jim Carstairs and are convinced he has nothing to do with either incident," Drake said. "After all the threats he's made and the fact that he was here today, I don't see how they can possibly dismiss him as a suspect."

"But from what you told me, wasn't he apologetic and contrite?" Holly asked.

"That could have easily been an act." Drake shrugged. "But I must let you get busy, or we won't have any late weather."

Holly smiled absently as he left her office, for her mind was churning with other possibilities. Suddenly she knew why she didn't think she was in any real danger.

Denise Warren had to be behind the entire mystery. Drake would probably fire her if she mentioned her theory, she thought resentfully. His precious Denise was perfect, and he would point out coldly that Denise hadn't been there when the weathercock was sprayed or when the doll was stolen.

But Denise had been only inches away from Holly

when she had fallen on the dance floor. *Tripped*, she corrected herself. And Denise had threatened to get rid of Holly.

Denise was probably behind the telephone calls, too. She must have an accomplice here at the television station. An angry knot began to gather inside Holly.

The entire thing was simply a ploy to force her to quit her job! Denise could save her efforts. Holly had no intention of quitting. Now she must stop playing detective and get her mind on the weather.

When she called the Weather Bureau, she discovered that a heavy fog was rolling in due to high humidity and southwesterly winds. The fog wouldn't lift before the middle of Saturday morning.

By the time the news and weathercasts were over, the fog had cut visibility to less than a quarter of a mile.

"Drive carefully," Drake said. "I'll be behind you, but be sure not to lose sight of my headlights."

The fog gave an eerie, ghostly feeling to the night, and she was glad that Drake was following her car, even though she knew now that she was in no physical danger. Her heart sank when she remembered that Drake would be with Denise tomorrow to shoot the commercials in the Wichita Mountains.

The fog would be gone in plenty of time not to interfere with the shooting of the commercials. Holly couldn't be mean enough to hope the fog wouldn't lift. Not even to thwart Denise.

There was practically no traffic, and with Drake's Ramcharger so closely behind her, it was as if the two of them were the last people in the world, completely enclosed in a bubble of white, misty light. She began to feel light-headed and disoriented, so that she had to concentrate carefully on her driving. She couldn't even be sure she would know where to turn. But Drake must have a better sense of direction, because she heard a loud honk and realized that she was about to miss the turnoff toward home.

Holly had supposed that Drake would continue on toward his own home when she made the turn down the lane to drive the half-mile, but he continued to follow her. Henry's car was in the drive, and she was glad that Fran hadn't been alone tonight.

The porch light that Fran had left on for her looked like a small golden moon suspended in the darkness. Drake, walking toward her with the fog moving about him, took on the appearance of a ghostly specter.

She shivered as that feeling came over her again that the two of them were the only people in the world. He said nothing, but simply took her hand as she got out of her car.

Their two hands were almost chilled from the dampness, but nonetheless, warmth spread in undulating waves from her fingertips through her entire body. The pressure of his hand on hers increased and her breath came unevenly. Her body came alive with a throbbing sweetness so intense that she could summon no arguments or defenses against it.

Suddenly she was in his arms, not knowing how it had happened. She clung to him while his hands moved over her shoulders, her arms and back. Then she felt his lips brushing her cheek and, finally, kissing the throbbing pulse at her throat. Her own hands reached to caress his face. She thought she would burst from the burning ache inside her, and her own lips eagerly sought his.

Holly heard his longing groan as their lips came together and his mouth explored hers, warm and expert, until at last their hearts beat in the same rhythm.

If only this moment could go on forever. But the kiss ended, leaving her more shaken than she could have thought possible. She could only lean weakly against his chest while his hands gently smoothed her hair.

"When we sealed a bargain, I didn't know it would lead to this," he said, his voice husky.

Still she couldn't speak, but looked up at him and tried to smile, pulling away and hoping she could stand without his support.

Was he apologizing for the kiss? She couldn't trust herself to speak, nor did she even know what to say. Was this all her doing? Out of her longing, had she thrown herself into his arms?

She didn't know, but he was looking at her strangely. "Don't worry, little sprite," he said, his voice tender. "It's going to be all right."

Suddenly she was miserable. Nothing was ever going be all right, for she knew that she was hopelessly, almost uncontrollably in love with him, and he couldn't possibly feel the same way about her.

She wanted to hide her face from him, sure that she was revealing her naked feelings. How disgusted he would be if he knew that she wanted to attach such importance to simply the mood of the moment.

Somehow she managed a shaky "Good night" and hoped he didn't guess how she felt.

13
ᚷᚷᚷᚷᚷᚷᚷᚷᚷᚷᚷ

May my heart be with me in the House of Hearts.

In her dream, Holly could hear herself saying the words over and over. She couldn't see anything, but she could hear clearly and her voice sounded as if she were in a cave, her words echoing back to her ears. She listened, trying to see into the total blackness, mesmerized and unable to move.

May my heart be with me in the House of Hearts.

Then abruptly her dream was filled with a brilliant light and she was at least nine feet tall, standing on a mountaintop and holding a bird in her hand. The bird had a human head. Her head!

She woke, a scream stifled in her throat and her entire body rigid with fear. Then slowly the familiar objects in her bedroom began to reassure her. The mahogany Queen Anne highboy, her old-fashioned tester bed, and her patchwork quilt with its many blocks from dresses of her childhood.

She wasn't nine feet tall and there was no bird

with his head cradled in the palm of her hand. She breathed a sigh of relief, but she was troubled by her dream and wondered where such dream material came from.

She looked at the clock on her bedside table. It was only five o'clock. But she was wide-awake, so she decided to slip downstairs and quietly make the coffee. Quickly she threw off her nightgown and got into jeans and shirt.

Surprised, she found the coffee already brewed and Fran comfortably seated at the kitchen table with pen, triangle, rulers, and paper, doing some sort of sketch. Holly gratefully poured a cup of the steaming coffee.

"My goodness, another early bird," Fran said.

Holly shuddered. "Don't say 'bird,'" she said, and told Fran about her dream. "I can't imagine what caused such a dream."

"What were you thinking about before you went to sleep?" Fran asked.

"The birds in Drake's chimney," she said, but didn't tell Fran that she had been thinking that anyone who was so tenderhearted with baby birds would certainly be gentle with a human who was obviously in love with him.

His innate compassion would explain why he had said that it would be all right. But her embarrassment would make it difficult to face him again.

"Birds in the chimney, hence the bird," Fran said, "and the House of Hearts is out of Egyptian mythology. Remember the book I was reading only a few weeks ago?" Fran stopped her sketching and got up to fill her own coffee cup. "I told you about the

Egyptian who had died. He held a bird in his hand with a human head that represented his soul. He pleaded for his heart to go with him."

"I do remember," Holly said thoughtfully. "And you told me about the Judgment Hall where hearts were weighed."

"Judged by Osiris, the ancient Egyptian god of the lower world and judge of the dead."

"I just hope my heart wasn't weighed and found wanting," Holly quipped. "I'm glad to know that my dream has some basis in logic, and that I didn't just tap into some reincarnational past."

Fran laughed. "Off with you," she said. "I'm trying to do a sketch for Henry of his latest idea for a wind-energy machine."

Holly chuckled. "Henry doesn't seem too retired. Wind energy, dollhouses, and reconstructing the Civil War. When does he ever find time to farm?"

"He's a busy man, all right," Fran said fondly; and then, wistfully, "So busy I'm amazed that he ever finds time for me."

"You're his battery charger," Holly said with her own wistfulness. "He looks at you and lights up."

She wished that she could provide some such spark for Drake, but she knew that could never be. Taking a last sip of her coffee, she placed her cup beside the coffeemaker. She'd have another cup later. "I'm going for a walk," she said.

Fran looked up from her sketching. "In this fog?"

Holly had forgotten the fog, but now that she'd had the idea, she didn't intend to be deterred. "I won't go far, and I'll take a flashlight."

When she opened the back door and stepped out into the murky morning, she didn't turn on the flashlight. She preferred to walk along and feel herself the center of a world that had narrowed to a circle of visibility that covered only a few feet.

She spotted the bright point on the fog's horizon and wondered briefly why it was called a fog dog. Her arms were swinging back and forth as she walked briskly. Soon her arms were covered with beads of moisture while the rest of her, although damp and clammy, was dry. The moisture must be caused by some sort of air displacement.

She speculated on this idea, knowing it was to keep her thoughts away from the real reason for her walk. Without consciously directing her steps, she was fully aware that she was making a wide circle around the house to reach the spot where Drake had held her in his arms and, if only for a moment, had given way to an explosion of attraction between them. He would have to admit he had felt the skyrockets, too, even if she had pushed her way into his arms.

She stood in that spot now, rubbing the moisture from her arms, living again that moment with every fiber of her being. For her it had stripped away the last vestige of the thin shell around her heart, a slender encasement that had kept her from knowing her true feelings for Drake.

But, standing there, immersed in the memory, she knew with a sickening certainty that he had only been responding, as any man would have, to her own yearnings.

She began walking again, moving her feet

woodenly, and shivering more from her thoughts than from the fog that pressed on her now like a physical weight. There was no way she could undo the fact that she had revealed too much to him.

Why hadn't she stiffened and turned away, rather than melting into his arms? But she didn't want to change that short time with him, because it might be all the love that she would ever know.

The television station, the weathercock, and the stolen doll seemed far away. It was as if it involved someone else, not Holly Meriweather. She was in danger, all right, but the danger was from her own feelings.

As she rounded the corner of the house, deep inside a world of her own, she heard a voice calling her name. The call sent chills through her, and it sounded as if some disembodied spirit were pleading with her. Then she knew the call was from Fran and hurried as fast as she could. Morning light had made some headway into the fog, and it must be close to six o'clock.

She called to Fran, letting her know she had heard her.

"Drake's on the phone," Fran called back.

Holly stopped and sucked in her breath, her legs weak and threatening to buckle under. Whatever could he want at this hour of the morning?

Fran held the door open for her to enter, and said, "He's really in a snit at your being out in this fog. I swear you've cast a spell over that man."

Don't I wish, Holly thought. Then with a huffy swish of her head, she set her jaw. What she did at six o'clock in the morning was none of his business, but then, thinking he might really care and seeing his face at the other end of the telephone, she said, "Good morning," very tenderly.

"How could you be outside before daylight in a thick fog?" he asked indignantly. "You could be in danger, and that person could be lurking around. Really, you need a keeper!"

If Drake were her keeper, she wouldn't mind. "I can very well take care of myself," she said.

"I see very little evidence of it," he snapped.

Her ears stung at his words, but he still hadn't told her why he was calling so early. Finally his grumbling ceased.

"Our announcer for the commercials in the mountains has waked up with laryngitis. He can scarcely speak above a whisper," Drake said. "I hate to call you on your day off, but could you possibly do the announcing?"

"Of course," she said, inwardly torn between delight and despair that she would be with him today after all.

He was pleased. "And you'll need to be camera-presentable," he said. "Wear that outfit you wore to the barbecue, the one with fringe. You looked like a tiny Pocahontas. An Indian maiden in the mountains would be the greatest."

She couldn't stop her heart singing, but then he said, "Holly, about last night, I hope—"

She interrupted. "Please, Drake, it would be better if we just say it never happened."

It was hard to keep her voice light, knowing he was going to say that he hoped she wasn't going to take their encounter seriously. Straightening her shoulders, she raised her body as tall as she could.

"That's what you want, to pretend it never happened?" He sounded offended.

Of course he was miffed that she hadn't completely succumbed to his charms. He must be accustomed to women swooning at his feet. On the other hand, he must surely be relieved that she wasn't going to be a problem.

"Would you like for me to meet you at the television station?" she asked, firm and businesslike.

"Absolutely not. This fog won't be lifting for a while, so I'll pick you up. Can you be ready in an hour?"

"I'll be waiting," she said.

As she dressed in the navy denim prairie skirt and frontier shirt, it seemed a lifetime ago since she'd worn it to Drake's party. It was now clean and free from the marks of her spill on the dance floor.

Her heart ached from the memories she had already accumulated, and her face burned thinking of the way she had flung herself into Drake's arms only last night.

He needn't be concerned about that, though. Today he would meet a new Holly, one that was immune to Drake Wimberly.

But she was nervous at seeing him again, so when she was dressed, she decided to wait outside the house. Restlessly she paced the distance between the porch and the gate. Finally she spotted the headlights of Drake's Ramcharger piercing through the lightening fog.

Quickly, not waiting for him to get out and help her, she climbed in beside him. Would he make any reference to the previous night? She needn't have wondered, because he launched immediately into a discussion of the reason for their trip to the mountains.

"This furniture store has never used television before, so the commercials are very important to us and to Denise."

Holly had expected they would pick up Denise, but Drake told her that Denise would lead the caravan of the furniture truck and the van with the camera crew and equipment. "We'll meet them in front of the wildlife-refuge office," he finished.

Drake drove carefully, and Holly looked ahead as the fog slowly lifted. Soon the Wichita Mountains could be seen in front of them, a majestic violet maze through the haze of morning.

The solitude of the wildlands was very appealing, and she thought of the buffalo, longhorn cattle, and deer that roamed free in the timbered mountainsides and gulches that ran beside the mountains. Was it the beauty of this slice of Oklahoma or Drake's impersonal attitude that caused the ache inside her? She only half-listened as he talked about the places his off-the-road vehicle had been. Then she realized that he was talking about the machines and the environment.

"The vehicles are capable of causing lasting damage to the land," he said, "killing vegetation and generally mangling what took nature aeons to evolve."

Feeling she should contribute something, she asked, "Then it's best to keep them on designated roads and trails."

"Mostly, that's true." He nodded. "ORV owners need to learn how to drive to preserve the land. Muddy tracks, such as those along a riverbank, will be washed away when heavy rains raise the river's level." Drake looked sideways at Holly, no doubt to see if she was listening. "In deep claylike mud, vehicle tracks can be baked by the sun into permanent molds and last for many years. Even driving across fresh spring grass leaves tracks that won't soon disappear."

"What about riverbeds?" she asked.

"That's okay, dry washes, too, because they're free of vegetation. Tracks across sand dunes will disappear with the next wind."

Holly was getting interested in the conversation, but they had reached the wildlife refuge, so Drake pulled into a parking space.

Suddenly there was silence between them. The fog that was almost gone seemed to have transferred itself into an invisible barrier. She gazed at the sprawling forests of tall evergreens, and now that the off-the-road vehicle subject had been exhausted, she could think of nothing to say.

After what must have been several minutes, Drake reached over and touched her hand. "Holly . . ." he said softly.

Quickly she withdrew as if burned, clenching both hands together in her lap. With a shrug he stopped whatever he had intended to say and stared past her toward the scenic view.

She shifted her gaze to search the road for the rest of their party. For once, she'd even be glad to see Denise.

14

Holly hadn't long to wait. Denise's sporty Fiat came into view, followed by the television station's van, and only seconds later, the truck loaded with the furniture for the commercials. Drake must have been really impatient for the rest to arrive. He wasted no time jumping from the Ramcharger and quickly making his way to Denise.

Watching him walk away, Holly decided his moving toward Denise and away from her was very symbolic. A tear came in her eye, but she brushed it away with a slapping movement of her hand. She watched him open the car door and help Denise alight. Smiling up at him, Denise took his arm and they walked together toward the van.

Bryan, Nelson, and the rest of the crew were milling about with paper cups in their hands. If they were drinking coffee, Holly would certainly like a cup of her own. With this dull and listless feeling, she needed something to pick her up.

Resolutely, she disembarked from the Ramcharger, greeted various members of the crew, and ran headlong into Nelson Sternum. He raked his eyes over her without speaking when she said good morning. She hurried past him and at last located a thermos of coffee inside the van.

After pouring a cup, she turned to find herself inches away from Nelson's face, his eyes boring into her. She shivered. He made her very uncomfortable. Raising a finger, he shook it in her face. "One day, lady, one day . . ." he said, and walked away from her.

Whatever did he mean? She couldn't tell whether he was attracted to her or hated her. He did such queer things.

She must have a talk with him soon. His strange behavior had to stem from something more than her withering glance the first time she saw him. She didn't want to be worrying about her relationship with a member of the crew.

There were enough other problems to be concerned with. Damaged weathercock, a stolen doll, and now, worst of all, her feelings for Drake.

Walking back to the car, she had to pass the spot where Drake and Denise were talking. She heard Denise say brightly, "I'll leave my car here and ride with you the rest of the way."

"Sorry," Drake answered. "The backseat is loaded with our lunch."

Holly saw Denise frown. "I really want to talk with you." She pouted. "Holly can drive my car."

"That's really not a good idea," he said. "I doubt that Holly would want to drive someone else's car around these twisting mountain roads."

Holly wished that Drake wanted to be alone with

her, but remembering the strain between them except for impersonal talk, she rather imagined that he simply didn't trust her to drive Denise's car.

Realizing she was eavesdropping, Holly started to move away. Denise spotted Holly and glared at her venomously. Without speaking to Holly, Denise turned back to Drake. "I wish our original announcer hadn't buckled under," she said clearly. "Holly is so inexperienced, I'm afraid we'll have trouble."

Now Holly did walk swiftly toward the Ramcharger, not wanting to hear Drake's reply. Quickly she climbed back into the safety of Drake's vehicle, huddling in the seat, and sipped at the coffee she had hoped would make her feel better.

By the time Drake joined her, she was feeling desolate, lonely, and almost angry. Obviously knowing that she had heard Denise's remarks, he said, "Denise is a little uptight. Gandy's Furniture is a new account, you know, and the commercials are very important."

Holly tried to smile reassuringly, but said nothing. He looked at her when she failed to reply. "You'll do fine," he said.

"I intend to," she said, and although she had vowed to be cooperative, she was afraid her tone of voice had been haughty.

Both were silent as Drake drove carefully through the mountains, leading the caravan. A deer darted across the road only a hundred yards in front of them, and Drake slowed his speed, although he was already driving very slowly. Minutes later, around a bend in the road, Drake brought the vehicle to a stop.

"This ought to be an ideal spot to shoot the commercials."

It was an area where short grass grew and the land slanted upward. Trees formed a semicircle around the scene. The sky, backdropping the mountains, was now a bright blue, with only a few small clouds drifting here and there. It did seem to be the perfect spot to place the furniture in a natural setting, Holly thought, as the other cars stopped behind them and the furniture truck drove in front of Drake's Ramcharger.

Toward the end of the second commercial, Holly realized that Denise's attitude had changed. Not once had she criticized Holly's performance. In fact, Holly noticed that Denise had seemed distracted and scarcely aware of what was going on.

Of course, Holly had to admit, the camera instructions had been explicit and well-thought-out. Holly's copy, too, was simple and direct. That could account for the departure in Denise's usual critical attitude. But Denise still appeared to be tense, and several times Holly had watched her eyes dart about as if looking for something or someone.

Even during the lunch break, Denise sat apart and didn't cling to Drake as usual. Holly noticed that Denise only nibbled at her food. Holly, however, was ravenous after her morning's work, and sitting on a boulder, unashamedly devoured ham-and-cheese sandwiches, several tomato slices, and large helpings of the potato salad and beans. Not even Drake, sitting on the short grass nearby, took the edge off her appetite.

The "back-to-nature" atmosphere and the fresh

mountain air could have contributed to her hunger. And although she was certain Arrowhead was sweltering in the heat and unusually high humidity, it didn't seem too hot here. Idly, intent on her food, she listened to Drake's and Bryan's conversation about editing the commercials.

When she finished the last bit of food on her plate, Drake looked up at her, his hazel eyes lighting up with that familiar teasing glint. His remark, though, was to Bryan. "Do you think the camera will pick up the extra pounds that Holly added during lunch?"

A blush warmed her face, and Bryan laughed. Not that it would have lessened her food intake, but she hadn't been aware that Drake was watching her. She looked into his eyes and managed a smile.

Suddenly her resentment toward him and the constraint that had developed between them was gone. A mellow feeling settled somewhere in her solar plexus, and the tightness that had been there dissolved.

Why not simply enjoy being with Drake? Who knew what the future might hold?

With a light heart she went back to work, and the afternoon commercials were even better than the morning ones. When the last commercial was over, Holly closed her eyes for a moment and thanked the mountains for a beautiful day. Now she looked forward to riding home alone with Drake.

The last piece of furniture had been loaded into the furniture truck and the camera equipment moved into the van when Denise's disappearance was noticed.

"I know she was here at the end of the last commercial, because she said it was a wrap," Holly said, but didn't add that Denise acted as if she didn't even care one way or the other. Holly was surprised that no one else had noticed Denise's strange attitude.

"That's the last time I remember seeing her, too," Bryan said.

"The rest of you can stand here and do nothing," Nelson Sternum said, "but I'm going to look for her." He whirled and took off on a trail that led up the mountains, calling her name.

Drake looked grim, but spoke calmly. "I'm sure that she has only taken a walk, but her judgment is poor to walk off and tell no one." He suggested that they split up, each taking one of the several trails up the mountainside. "Holly and I will take the trail to the right," he finished.

As the two of them walked along, Holly grew breathless, more from Drake's guiding hand on her arm than from the rocky, short-grassed terrain that became a steeper and steeper incline toward the mountain's timberline.

Occasionally Drake stopped, cupped his hands to his mouth, and called Denise's name. It was the second time they halted on the trail that Drake took Holly's small hand in his larger one.

The masculine pressure of his fingers entwined in hers sent ripples up her arm to her spine, setting off a joy inside her that was hard to contain. *Stop it, Holly,* she said to herself. *Enjoy, but not too much.* Of course, she knew that Drake was concerned about Denise's wandering off, but certainly not with the frantic apprehension that Nelson Sternum had shown.

Once again Drake halted their progress up the steepening path. He called out several times, and this brought an answer. Denise's voice came weakly from behind a bush off the trail.

"Help! Oh, please, help!"

They found her quickly, lying on the ground, raised on one elbow. Undoubtedly she wanted to protect her perfect hairdo, Holly thought cynically.

Denise looked upward at Drake pathetically. "I just knew you'd be the one to find me," she said. "I stumbled against the bush, lost my footing, and fell here." Her expression became even more droopy. "I . . . I can't get up. It's my back." She moved her hand to a spot in the middle of her back.

Drake knelt beside her, and now his expression was worried. "Are you in pain?"

"Oh, yes, particularly when I move the least little bit," she said, twisting her face in a grimace to prove it.

"I'm not sure you should be moved before a doctor sees you," he said.

Her face showed alarm. "I'm sure I'll be all right in a little while if you'll carry me down the trail," she said pleadingly.

I'll bet you'll be all right, Holly agreed silently. Not only was every hair in place, but even her beige pantsuit wasn't mussed the way it surely would have been if she had taken the tumble she described. Holly was positive the supposed fall was only a trick to get Drake's attention.

It worked. He carefully picked up Denise from the

ground. Holly watched in disgust as Denise twined her arms around his neck.

"I'm fine in your arms. The way you're carrying me, my back doesn't hurt a bit." Denise was whispering, but Holly heard her. Then Denise looked over Drake's shoulder and shot Holly a triumphant look. As if that wasn't enough, Denise kissed him on the cheek and said coyly, "Thank you for rescuing me."

"I'm an easy mark for a damsel in distress," Drake replied. "Sure you're comfortable?"

"Heavenly," she said. "That hard ground isn't the best place for an injured back."

"We'll go down slowly. If your back starts hurting, let me know." Although his attention was completely on Denise, he did call back to tell Holly to watch her step.

Trailing behind them she was glad she'd put on boots instead of the moccasins she'd worn to the party. She felt cheated and blinked back the tears that were threatening to cascade down her cheeks. She *could* cry all she liked. Drake wouldn't even notice. Walking down the path wasn't all that easy without Drake's support. Going up had been much faster. Twice she almost lost her footing. On the way down, she could hear the murmur of voices, but could catch only a word here and there.

At last they were back at their starting point and were greeted with shouts of "Bravo" at Drake's finding Denise. His face was showing the strain of carrying his human package. Denise was tall and big-boned, so she couldn't have been that light to carry, even for someone as strong as Drake.

Holly couldn't believe it when he asked Nelson Sternum to open the door of his Ramcharger. Where did he expect Holly to ride? The backseat was filled with coolers, lunch baskets, a bean pot, and the remains from their midday meal.

Any leftover joy went out of Holly when Denise triumphantly took Holly's place in the vehicle.

Drake then turned to Holly. "Nelson will drive Denise's car, Holly, and you can ride with him," he said, completely dismissing her.

She had much rather ride with Bryan and the crew in the van if she couldn't be with Drake. But she didn't argue, and followed meekly behind Nelson to Denise's car. Morosely she opened the car door and got in beside Nelson, who was already behind the wheel.

He'd made no move to open the door for her. It didn't matter, as she was capable of opening her own doors. Then, without asking her leave, he put the top down.

Actually, Holly was delighted. The breeze would feel good on her hot face, and she was lucky that the wind couldn't possibly do more than tangle her short curly hair. Briefly she wondered if Denise ever took the chance of damaging her perfectly coiffed hair by putting the top down.

Nelson pulled away ahead of the Ramcharger and furniture truck, driving rather too fast along the twisting roads. Determined not to be nervous, she leaned against the back of the seat and shut her eyes, relishing the warm air blowing on her face and twisting her hair. But she did breathe a sigh of relief when they reached the open highway and the speed was less dangerous.

Finally Nelson spoke, but it was a grumble. "Mr. Drake Wimberly is pretty high-handed to put Denise in his car. She could have ridden in her own car with me."

Holly agreed, but didn't say so. Obviously Drake wasn't the only one who preferred Denise's company to hers. She would like to tell Nelson that since he was stuck with her, he might as well make the best of it. After all, Drake was the boss.

"Scarcely anyone appreciates Denise's talent and beauty," Nelson said. Holly sighed inwardly. Apparently she was in for a summary of Denise's charms. Nelson continued, "Denise should be in front of the camera, not behind it." Then, with a slam of his hand against the steering wheel, he said, "If Drake was determined to have a female announcer, it should have been Denise."

Holly opened her eyes and looked at him, appalled that he would have the audacity to express such a thing to the station's first and only female announcer.

She tried to keep her voice light when she replied, "Perhaps Denise doesn't care about on-camera work." Since she was alone in the car with Nelson, she didn't want to antagonize him.

"Denise needs to be taken care of," he said stubbornly. "She needs someone to look out for her interests."

Like a cobra, Holly thought. Poor Nelson.

She was beginning to feel sorry for him and to understand why he didn't like her. But Denise only used people like Nelson. Drake was Denise's target, and her marksmanship was good, Holly decided, thinking of the trick she'd used to get to ride back to town with Drake.

With a sinking heart, she pictured Denise cuddled beside Drake, the beautiful sunset behind them. How lovely Denise must look to Drake in the dimming twilight. Holly scolded herself for dwelling on such thoughts. Wasn't it bad enough, just knowing they were together?

Suddenly, without warning, Nelson slowed his speed. He reached across the seat, and Holly felt his fingers close tightly around her wrist.

"Nelson!" she cried, trying to pull away. But his fingers held her wrist tightly, as if he might break her tiny bones. Then, as suddenly as he had grabbed her wrist, he released it and slowed the car's speed even more.

"See," he said, pointing to a lonely, narrow side road barely visible in the gathering dusk. "I could take you down that road—"

"You wouldn't dare," Holly interrupted, rubbing her wrist to bring the feeling back, her entire body trembling with fright.

Nelson laughed. "You're right, I wouldn't," he said, "but I scared you, didn't I?"

"Certainly you frightened me," she said. "Don't ever, ever do that again."

"Oh, I'll never do that again!"

In spite of his sarcastic reassurance, Holly could hardly wait to get home, out of Denise's car, and away from him. Was this his idea of a joke?

15

ᘯᘯᘯᘯᘯᘯᘯᘯᘯᘯᘯ

Nelson increased his speed again, and this time Holly was glad. The faster he drove, the quicker she would be home. And she had to admit that Denise's Fiat was a smooth-running little jewel. Nelson whistled a happy tune and seemed to have gained some kind of joy in scaring the daylights out of her.

Suddenly, nearing the television station, an overpowering urge came over her to stop and check the news wire for weather information. Was she having a hunch that bad weather was developing somewhere? Henry said that every good weathercaster sooner or later developed a sixth sense.

She remembered his saying many times, "Meteorology is a science, but it's also an art." His face would light up and his eyes would sparkle whenever he talked about the mystical aspect in weather forecasting.

"That's why computers don't have it all," he said. "You can't make a computer do art. And meteorology is an art because of the feeling you get."

Her imagination might be on a rampage, but as much as she wanted to be home and away from Nelson, she had to get him to stop at the television station.

She spoke quietly. "Nelson, I need to stop at the station for just a minute."

"But I want to get you home and check on Denise," he protested.

"I'm sure Drake is taking very good care of Denise," Holly said dryly, an unhappy picture of Drake and Denise overriding for a moment her intensity to check the weather. Then she said in as commanding a voice as she could muster, "It is imperative that I check the weather, and it will delay us for only a moment."

With a reluctant grumble Nelson turned the Fiat into the station's drive and parked at the back of the building. "I'll wait here," he said sulkily.

Holly was out of the car, inside the building, and racing toward the newsroom. There was no one around, and the wire machine was quiet, but yards of paper streamed from the black monster. Obviously the ten-o'clock-news crew had not arrived for the Saturday-night run.

She ripped the news stories from the machine and looked around for the steel ruler that was used to cut the stories apart. This would take longer than she had planned, and Holly hoped fervently that Nelson wouldn't drive off and leave her. She wouldn't be surprised if he did.

Hastily scanning the stories, she tore them apart as she read, her heart in her throat. The staccato clatter of the machine started when she was only about a third of the way through the news stories. More stories were now coming over the wire. Carefully folding the remaining paper, almost fearfully she walked back to the machine.

When she read the story that was coming through, she could scarcely believe her eyes. She had expected perhaps thunderstorms and hail developing, but it was more. Air Force reconnaissance planes had been sent out to check on a possible hurricane close to the Bahamas.

Tremors that her body could scarcely contain pounded inside her. No one would believe her at this point, not even Henry, since it wasn't happening to him, but she had a gut feeling that Arrowhead would experience violent weather, possibly more violent than this area had ever experienced.

From this moment on, she would be spending much time at the Weather Bureau, checking the weather charts and keeping track of the developing storm. If she did her job right, lives and property might be saved. But for the moment, she must keep such thoughts to herself, or else be branded as a lunatic. How grateful she was to Henry and her years of training with him!

"If you're dedicated to your work," he had told her often, "this intuitive sensing of future weather occurs to most forecasters who are not truly involved with the mathematics of meteorology."

She breathed deeply to quiet herself, and when she emerged from the building, Nelson was pacing like a caged animal around the Fiat.

"I told you I was in a hurrry," he said icily. "Denise could be badly hurt."

Holly doubted it, but apologized meekly and thanked him for waiting. Fortunately he didn't question her about the weather news. In a very short time she was on her doorstep and waving good-bye to the Fiat as Nelson whirled the car around in a swirl of dust.

Kurt's car and Henry's were parked in front of the house. She expected that Henry would be there, but she was surprised to know that Kurt was here. He didn't make a habit of coming out without telephoning first.

Probably he was curious to know if there was news of Fran's missing doll. Briefly she wondered if there had been any news.

Inside the door and into the hall, Holly could hear Henry and Fran once again fighting the Civil War. Apparently only Kurt heard her entrance.

He slipped into the hall where she stood and put his arms around her. She leaned her head against his shoulder, and his closeness was a warm and comfortable cloak around her. But when he tilted her face toward his and kissed her on the lips, she could not respond.

"Oh, Holly . . ." He said her name tenderly but sadly.

How simple everything would be if she could return his love. How kind he was. He kissed her gently on the forehead and moved her head back to his shoulder as if he understood.

Of course, he *didn't* understand, because he couldn't possibly know how she felt about Drake. How would Kurt react if she told him that she could never return his love? It wasn't fair not to tell him, but somehow she couldn't find the strength to do so.

She pulled away, but reached for his hand and

smiled. They stood for a moment listening to the lively conversation in the den.

"Henry, Henry," Fran said in exasperation.

"But it's true," Henry protested. "Governor John Jones Pettus of Mississippi did not fit the stereotype of southern governors."

"So?" Fran retorted flippantly.

"So if the Confederate government had listened to him, Vicksburg wouldn't have fallen." Henry paused. "Jefferson Davis was his cousin, you know."

"I don't know a thing about the war," Fran replied, "but from what you've told me, though, Governor Pettus may have been a fire-eater, but he was mostly interested in the welfare of Mississippi."

"He also knew the value of the Mississippi River and the importance of its control," Henry retorted.

"Whatever, I'm glad the South didn't win," Fran said.

"That's because your ancestors were Yankees," Henry said.

"Damn Yankees," Fran said firmly, and as usual, their verbal battle ended in laughter.

Holly and Kurt entered the den and joined in the merriment. "You're a good sport, Henry," Holly said. "I don't see how you put up with all of us who don't know a thing about your just cause."

"I love you anyway," Henry said. "And how was your day?"

Holly recounted the day's events, carefully leaving out her suspicions that Denise hadn't taken a tumble. When she told about stopping by the television station to check the weather, she simply stated that a hurricane appeared to be brewing off the Bahamas.

She longed to tell Henry that she might be having a weather forecaster's hunch that had nothing to do with what other forecasters might say or with a computer's logic. But now, in the normalcy of her own home, she was beginning to doubt her intuition, and the strong feeling was fading. She still couldn't resist asking Henry one question.

"I'd like to pick your brain on something," she said.

"While you're picking," Fran said, "I'll put dinner on the table." She got up from the couch and disappeared toward the kitchen.

When Fran was out of sight, Holly asked, "How long before a weather disaster might a forecaster pick up on it?" Although she tried to keep her voice casual and academic, Henry looked at her sharply.

"I don't suppose there's any set rule," he said. "Who knows what the human mind can do? Fran will remember that I was in Cuba before Hurricane Camille." He paused and took a pen and notepad from his shirt pocket. "I can talk better with a pen." He drew a rough sketch of the coastline and a line across the gulf. "When the hurricane was just a tropical depression, I drew a line like this, forcasting landfall. That was a number of days before it hit."

He interrupted his story to fix a round of drinks and pour Holly a small glass of white wine. "All we had to go on was radio data, no computers. From a satellite read-out chart I could actually see the little glob in my mind that was the tropical depression and follow it mentally to landfall." Henry's eyes were glowing with the memory. "It's a thrill, I can tell you, when that happens."

"Maybe one day that will happen to me," Holly said wistfully.

"It will, it will," Henry said, watching her carefully. She could tell he wanted to question her, but just then Fran announced that dinner was served.

Kurt, who had been listening quietly to the conversation, walked over to Holly to enter the dining room with her. His eyes on her were loving but determined, if she read the look correctly.

Oh, dear, she thought. *I must tell him soon that there's just no hope. Just as there's no hope for me in loving Drake.*

She was glad when he turned his attention to the delicious spaghetti, garlic toast, and green salad. Another of Fran's great meals, Holly concluded.

"By the way," Kurt said between bites. "We haven't told you, but the police think they know who stole the Jumeau doll and perhaps sprayed the weathercock with the red paint."

"Man or woman?" Holly asked.

"They won't say," Kurt replied, "but they're keeping a close watch on the suspect. Apparently they need more evidence and are just waiting for the person to make another move."

"I hope that move doesn't have anything to do with Holly," Fran said worriedly. "Even though she was with Drake today, I wasn't quite easy until she got home."

Holly smiled, appreciating her concern. If Denise was the suspect, there was very little harm she could do at the moment, considering that she was with

Drake and supposedly injured. Anyway, Holly was sure that Denise's managing a ride back with Drake was enough annoyance at the moment.

Annoyance was all that any of it amounted to. And if Denise could keep Drake away from Holly, there would be no more occurrences. It was entirely clear, too, that the moment Denise needed him, he had abandoned all interest in Holly's welfare.

She must put Drake out of her mind. The next week to ten days could be the most important of her life. If it wasn't her imagination and she was really experiencing a weather forecaster's sixth sense, her years of study and absorbing meteorological information could culminate in saving lives and property.

Then, in some strange way, her parents' death so many years ago from lack of warning would have gained a purpose. She simply had to keep a clear mind, unclouded by hopeless longing for a man who didn't love her.

It was after dinner and coffee in the den when she noticed that Kurt had been silent for a long time. He kept looking at her in a peculiar way, almost as though he was seeing her for the first time.

Finally Kurt spoke to Holly quietly. "I must talk with you," he said.

"Not tonight, Kurt," she said. "I'm very tired."

"Then tomorrow," he said firmly. She knew he wouldn't be put off.

"Come out tomorrow afternoon," she said. What could have put him into such an intent, unwavering mood?

She continued to wonder about Kurt's behavior

after he had gone. His eyes had been a darker gray than usual, and she sensed a turbulence behind them, seething like a tumultuous sea before a storm. Was it possible that he wanted to tell her he had found someone else?

Getting ready for bed, Holly examined how she would feel if Kurt no longer wanted to marry her. That would really be ironic, when only hours ago she had felt guilty about her own unrequited love for Drake. But was she really prepared to give up Kurt?

16
ರರರರರರರರರರ

Holly slept until far into Sunday morning. When she awakened, a hot stickiness had plastered her nightgown to her body, and through the glass door the sun shone with dazzling brilliance across her bed. She glanced at her clock ticking away the minutes. Eleven o'clock. What a waste to sleep away the day!

She sat up, descended the bed steps, and thrust her feet into the blue satin slides that matched her nightgown. For a moment she stood at the glass door looking out at the mountains and remembering how quickly Drake had turned from her to Denise. He hadn't even called to see if Holly had arrived

home safely. She hadn't checked to see if Denise
was badly hurt because she was absolutely sure Denise had faked that fall. Holly shrugged impatiently
away from the door.

She was going to get dressed, have a cup of coffee,
and head for the Weather Bureau. More reports
would certainly be in on the storm off the Bahamas.
She needed to be home before Kurt dropped by.

That promised to be an ordeal. She wasn't sure
how she'd feel if he wanted to tell her he'd found
someone else. It wasn't fair to expect him to always
be on hand, but she felt a definite pang at the
thought of losing her longtime friend. Kurt had always been in the background, a reassuring, steady-
ing comfort. Not a bit like Drake, who was so
bewildering, and who was clearly no more than
slightly attracted to her.

Wasn't it possible, even likely, that once she got
over her unlucky infatuation for Drake, she could
love Kurt? He was dear and kind, one of her favorite
people. Couldn't he be more?

The shower washed away some of her confusion
along with the uncomfortable stickiness. Dressing in
a yellow gauze blouse and matching three-tiered
skirt, she brushed her dark curls to a shining halo
and hurried downstairs.

A note was pinned to the bulletin board. *"Gone
with Henry to inspect the wind-power site—and then
who knows where else? Didn't want to awaken you.
Have a happy day."*

Whether that last was possible or not, Holly was
glad not to have to explain why she was going to the
Bureau on her day off. Besides, she preferred to see

Kurt alone, especially if whatever he was being so mysterious about turned out to be upsetting.

She pulled the Sunbird into the graveled driveway of the small flat-topped stucco building that housed the Weather Bureau. She sat for a moment gazing at the building while memories washed over her.

When she had first visited here, Henry had to lift her into his big high-backed swivel chair with its thick black cushion. Her feet dangled in midair, unable to reach the floor. She had measured the passage of time by the distance of her feet from the floor, until at last she was grown-up enough to sit comfortably with her feet almost flat on the tiled floor.

Long before that time, she had begun to understand such things as the vorticity charts and all the arrows and wavy lines that crossed and crisscrossed the weather maps, indicating wind directions and the movement of fronts.

Holly glanced at her watch. She had spent far too much time in reverie. Quickly she got out of the car and hurried up the winding sidewalk, through the wooden door, and into the huge square room.

Henry's big chair had been gone a long time, replaced by modern chrome-armed, short-backed chairs. Otherwise the room was very much the same, with the charts, maps, and notations hanging on the wall.

There was no one around when she walked in. Apparently the person on duty had slipped to the back for a cup of coffee. Wherever he was, she was glad to be alone to check the weather.

Her hunch was right.

The tropical depression had developed into Hurrican Andrew out over open water. Winds were rapidly increasing, moving northwest. If Andrew maintained its present headings, it would pass the Florida Keys and spread into the Gulf of Mexico within a few days.

The best meteorologists wouldn't predict the hurricane would cause any extremely bad weather in Arrowhead, but as she studied the information and mentally traced the path the storm might take, Holly was gripped with an unexplainable certainty that Arrowhead was in danger.

Such a prediction now would be absurd, but the foreboding presentment persisted as she drove home and went into the kitchen to make coffee for Kurt.

Trying to minimize the almost physical sense of threat, she chided herself sternly. Perhaps her anxiety over what Kurt might say was spilling over into her weather sensitivity. Just because her personal life was in chaos, did she have to imagine disasters for the town?

She'd keep a close eye on developments, but she had to rein in these fears over Hurricane Andrew or she'd be a wreck long before she could responsibly even mention her eerie conviction.

Kurt's familiar hearty knock sounded on the door as the last coffee dripped into the glass container. She opened the door to find him standing there with the same determined expression that had been in his face and eyes the night before. He looked crisply assured in a blue sport shirt and white slacks. His thick, wavy hair had been slightly mussed by the wind and slanted across his forehead.

Strange to feel awkward and unsure with Kurt. With a smile she felt to be falsely bright, she invited him in with a wave of her hand. "Coffee's just ready! And Fran's off with Henry, so we have the place to ourselves."

"Good." He practically marched inside. "If our confab doesn't go the way I think it should, I'm ready to rage and roar."

"That bad?" she teased.

He eyed her grimly. "I've decided it's time we faced up to some facts, young lady."

She didn't like the sound of that.

"Well, have Grand Ben's chair," she said. "That's a good place from which to issue solemn pronouncements. And let me bring the coffee. It sounds as if we're going to need it!"

Welcoming a few minutes' reprieve, she fled to the kitchen.

Surely she wasn't the type of female to say: *I may not want you, but I don't want anyone else to have you either.* But he had been around for so long, adoring her, always making her feel important. It wasn't easy to give that up.

Still, if Kurt had found someone to truly love him, she would bless him and wish him well regardless of the emptiness it might leave with her.

When she returned to the den with coffee, she was braced for what he had to say. She handed him the cup with two lumps of sugar.

"How long has it been since I walked off that seventh-grade football field and saw you standing on the sidelines?" He took a drink of the coffee and grinned at her. "I reached over and yanked a handful of your curly hair."

"And I slapped your face," she said with a remembering smile. "I wasn't all that angry, though. You made the winning touchdown."

"That was the beginning. I've never looked at another girl, at least not long."

Now he would tell her, she thought.

He was very serious when he spoke again. "All these things that have happened, the threatening notes and phone calls, it's made me know that something must be done about us."

"I don't understand," she said. Was he simply going to tell her that he intended to find another love?

Reaching in his pocket, he pulled out a small square burgundy velvet box. Flipping the box open, he passed it to Holly. She gasped, aghast at the size of the diamond, square cut and sparkling in a wide gold mounting.

"It's absolutely beautiful," she said.

So this was his way of telling her he had found someone else. Who was she? Saddened, for a moment Holly envied the one who would wear this ring, the one who could love Kurt and give him the affection he deserved.

"It's yours, I want you to wear it," he said.

"Mine!" She couldn't believe it.

"Here," he said, "let me put it on your finger."

"Oh, Kurt, you know I can't . . ." But even as she protested, he slipped the ring on the third finger of her left hand. She gazed at it, mesmerized.

"I know you think you don't love me enough to

marry me," he said quietly. "I'm only asking you to wear it, get accustomed to it, feel it on your finger, and think seriously about living your life with me. I must know that you're safe and taken care of. I want that someone who takes care of you to be me."

"You mean a trial engagement?" she asked.

"It needn't even be that. Not as far as you and I are concerned." He smiled at her reassuringly. "The ring is a symbol that you'll think seriously about marrying me."

"But everyone else would think we're engaged!"

"Would that be so bad?" he asked with a grin before he sobered. "Maybe you're already in love with another man?"

She couldn't look at him and lie, but neither could she admit that she was in love with a man who didn't love her. Why not be half-engaged to Kurt? Denise might leave her alone and let her work in peace. She wouldn't have to be embarrassed around Drake, constantly trying to hide how she felt about him. If he thought she was engaged to Kurt, Drake would quit playing games behind Denise's back. And Holly would try her best to be in love with Kurt and make it a real engagement.

He must have read the answer in her eyes. He stood up, leaned over, and kissed her gently. She twisted the ring around on her finger, feeling its strangeness there. Perhaps when she grew accustomed to it, she'd also feel comfortable about marrying Kurt.

After he had gone, she sat for a long time on the couch in Fran's place as though she might absorb a measure of her grandmother's levelheaded quietness.

What on earth would Fran say about Holly's engagement? Holly knew she would have to let Fran know exactly why she was wearing the ring. Fran would never believe that Holly had suddenly discovered that she loved Kurt and wanted to marry him.

Bemused, Holly sat wondering how various people would react to her "engagement." She still felt uneasy about it, especially when she thought of Drake. It would be a relief to talk it all over with Fran.

Holly hadn't heard a car pull in, but a knock came at the door. Had Fran forgotten her key? Opening the door, Holly stared in surprise at Drake, who looked back at her with an air of determination that equaled Kurt's.

In beige linen suit and dark brown shirt, Drake had that silver-screen appearance, but it was the searching look in his hazel eyes that sent her heart racing. Kurt's ring on her finger certainly hadn't affected her inner feelings yet.

Would it ever?

"Come in," she invited, surprised that she sounded so politely cordial.

"Just for a minute. I've had news on the stolen doll."

"Really?"

He grinned. "Give me some coffee and I'll tell you all I can."

She poured him a cup of the pungent brew and got another for herself, following him into the den. He had taken Grand Ben's chair. He looked very much at home when Holly returned and perched on the ottoman a few feet from Drake.

Would he notice the ring?

"First," he said, "I thought you'd be glad to know Denise only had a slight wrench to her back. She's up and around today."

"That's good." Holly couldn't sound enthusiastic but at least managed to keep her suspicions to herself.

Drake leaned forward. "Now, the doll. The police have made a thorough investigation. They think they know who took the doll and sprayed paint on the weathercock. It for sure wasn't Jim Carstairs."

"Whom do they suspect?"

"They're not saying yet." Drake frowned. "But you must be careful, Holly. Careful of everyone at the station till this is settled."

"Then it was someone at work?"

"Yes, but we don't know why," he growled. "There's apparently not enough evidence to charge the suspect. We'll have to wait for another move." His eyes were so concerned, his face so troubled, that she could scarcely keep from reaching over to touch him reassuringly.

"No one's been hurt," she reminded him.

He nodded as if he'd frequently been reciting those comforting words to himself. "All the same, I want you to be mighty careful. It's a shame to have to include everyone in this warning, but please don't leave there with anyone."

"Not even you?" she said, knowing she was flirting, but unable to resist.

When he reached across the short space between them and took her hand, she knew she shouldn't have teased. He had taken her left hand and cov-

ered it with his other hand. It was as if the ring on
her finger was on fire, so quickly did he take away
his fingers. She couldn't read the expression on his
face, because he was looking down at the ring.

"Kurt?" he said grimly.

"Of course," she whispered, aching to tell him that
it wasn't a real engagement. But she steeled herself
not to do so.

"Then I wish you every happiness," he said
formally, rising to leave.

When he was gone, she rubbed the hand that had
felt so right in his, then looked at Kurt's ring, her
heart sinking.

What had she done? Was there a chance, after all,
that Drake might care for her?

17

In the several days that followed, Holly had little
time to be concerned about her personal life. Although she saw Kurt or talked on the telephone with
him daily, he did not press her. He appeared confident that his ring on her finger would work its
magic.

There was very little talk at work about the missing Jumeau doll and who might be responsible for

its disappearance. Although she was wary of everyone as Drake had suggested, she couldn't believe that anyone she worked with was guilty. She was certain that Denise was truly behind the mysterious episodes.

Now that Holly was supposedly engaged, Denise was much friendlier and less critical of the commercials that Holly did for Denise's accounts. Holly didn't complain when she had to scream her way through a used-car spiel, shatter the windshield with a hammer, and announce that prices had been smashed. Although she knew that she had looked ridiculous and sounded even worse, she kept quiet.

Only Drake's constant cold formality took her mind off Hurricane Andrew as it moved with the relentless precision of a machine through the open waters of the Gulf of Mexico toward the Louisiana coastline. She was up early each morning, spending her free hours at the Weather Bureau tracking the storm and continuing inexplicably to feel that Arrowhead would experience bad weather as a result. Each day the humidity increased.

She couldn't believe the week had passed so swiftly. If only she could keep her mind off Drake and completely on the weather, maybe she could crystallize her feeling that really bad weather was going to hit. Then she could pinpoint a forecast.

It was on Monday when it happened. She was at the Weather Bureau early. If Hurricane Andrew didn't change its course, it would hit the Louisiana coastline in the next seventy-two hours. But something new had entered the weather picture. A front had developed in Oregon and a jet stream was pushing south. She studied the upper air data carefully. Her heart began to pound and the palms of her hands were moist.

Holly stood, looking at the charts. In her mind, she watched the movements, up and down. Her body was becoming a tool, absorbing not only what the charts said but also the entire motion of the atmosphere which permeated her entire being.

She visualized the weather moving, not only back and forth, but up and down, and as time worked with the weather, what was going to happen.

Ginning! She was really ginning. That was the word Henry used when he told her about such possibilities. It was like building a four-dimensional puzzle. She now had everything together. It was scary, but she knew it would happen just as she saw it now in her mind.

The front from Oregon was to the north of Arrowhead. She felt that Hurricane Andrew would stay on its present course and hit land somewhere close to Lake Charles, Louisiana. She could feel the thunderstorms that would come across in squalls and bands as the hurricane moved closer to Arrowhead and got mixed up with the Oregon frontal system.

In her mind she could see the twisty bands spiraling into the eyes of the hurricane. By then the eye would be disorganized, having lost its tropical characteristics. She could see it hitting the front to the west and moving back over the town, dragging the hurricane through with the front.

That's when the bad weather would hit. She was fearful, excited, even elated, all at the same time.

Regardless of what other forecasters might be saying at that time, Holly knew she could sound the warning in plenty of time for whatever evacuation might be necessary.

For now, she would still have to keep quiet. She couldn't go on the air with nothing but her sixth-sense forecast. It would be almost a twenty-four-hour-a-day job now to stay with the tracking of the front and the hurricane.

Holly reached the television station, her head and hands filled with enough information for scores of weathercasts instead of one at six o'clock. It would take all the time she had to condense the data into a five-minute report. And surely she could find a way to hint that there was a possibility of Arrowhead's receiving some effects of the hurricane and the front from Oregon.

It was dark and gloomy in her office, and she rushed to open the draperies. The room needed sunlight. Turning toward her desk, she couldn't believe her eyes. Sitting in the desk chair, upright, prim, and completely unharmed, was the Jumeau doll. She caught the doll in her arms, carrying it like a child. Heedless of several startled glances, she ran down the hall to Drake's office.

He was sitting at his desk with the office door open, intent on papers in front of him. He looked up when Holly entered the office, his startled gaze matching her own disbelief that the doll had been returned. His attention now was fully on her and the Jumeau as he awaited her explanation.

"I never expected this," he said when she finished.

"But it does change the picture. Now we really have no case against the person who took it."

"Who cares?" Holly laughed. "Fran will have her doll, and this must mean there'll be no more mysteries."

"I hope you're right." He brooded a moment before he shrugged and brightened. "Let me drop the doll off at Fran's. I'm going home for a little while, so it'll be no trouble."

"Fran'll give you a big hug," Holly said, handing him the Jumeau. Rising, he held it awkwardly against him, making such a ludicrous spectacle that Holly couldn't choke down her laughter.

After a startled glance, he chuckled and tugged a curl by her ear. His hand brushed her skin, sending a sweet warm shock through her.

"Hilarious, am I? Can I help it if I never played with dolls?"

"Live ones?" she dared.

"I've never tried to carry them around."

Fun and good fellowship flowed between them as they walked down the hall together. It was the first time since he'd noticed her ring that he'd dropped his standoffish manner, and Holly's heart sang. Stealing a sideways look, she decided that he was holding the doll in a more relaxed fashion and had a wistful flash of wondering how he'd look carrying a child of his own.

Pausing outside her office, he seemed worried again. "The danger may not be over," he warned. "Watch what you do, Holly. I feel responsible for you. If . . ."

Had she imagined it, or had his voice broken on

that last unfinished sentence? She twisted Kurt's ring on her finger.

How heavy it felt! As she sat at her desk trying to concentrate on the important job at hand, the ring became increasingly burdensome, transferring itself to a weight dragging at her heart. Finally, with a sigh, she removed the ring, wrapped it carefully in a handkerchief, and put the package in her coin purse to return to Kurt.

Marriage to him was completely out of the question. She was hopelessly in love with Drake Wimberly. Since marrying Drake was also out of the question, she had no choice but to devote herself wholeheartedly to her career. After all, hadn't Henry said that weather was a capricious and challenging lover?

Once again she turned with determination to her job. This time, with a decision firmly made, it was easier to become absorbed in her charts and notations.

18
∿∿∿∿∿∿∿∿∿∿∿

In the early hours of Wednesday morning, Hurricane Andrew hit landfall, as predicted, near Lake Charles, Louisiana. Luckily the major thrust of the storm was in the swamplands so that little property damage was done and no lives were lost. But as Henry said when Holly called him a report from the Weather Bureau, "It won't horse around now. It's going to keep on walking."

The storm did keep walking, headed toward Fort Worth, Texas. All forecasting indicated that Andrew would turn on a north recurve, bending toward the right, completely away from Arrowhead.

Not in Holly's mind, however. She was on a real high, having worked long hours without much sleep. But she wasn't sleepy or tired or even hungry. She seemed to be outside of herself, absorbing, expanding, feeling.

When Holly left the Weather Bureau to go to the television station, winds were from the southeast and there were no clouds, but she knew the atmosphere was pumping up moisture. And the humidity was unbearable.

Henry had mentioned the humidity when Holly talked with him. "We'll experience the kind of swampy heat that makes people half-mean," he said.

Of course, he didn't know that she was sure Arrowhead would get severe weather from this storm and the front. Or did he?

"Remember to try to see the winds, not just blowing horizontally, but with a vertical motion on the ground," he said. "Look at three dimensions, plus time, and you're in the fourth dimension of weathercasting."

Holly had been doing that. But after talking with Henry, she leaned back in her chair to rest her eyes for a moment. Other thoughts intruded on her weather speculations. Guiltily she remembered Kurt's ring in her purse, and she thought about Drake, wondering what he was doing at this moment. She must stop that kind of thinking and get back to her work.

Once she did, the afternoon passed swiftly. After the six-o'clock weathercast, she hurriedly ate a sandwich at home, scarcely tasting the ham and cheese, intent on getting to the Weather Bureau.

At the Weather Bureau, she again studied the upper air currents carefully, making her own interpretations. She felt herself absorbing again, feeling the expansion, and seeing in her mind more than was on the charts in front of her.

Clearly she saw what was going to happen. The jet stream from Oregon, becoming now more a north-south front, would roll through. At about that time, the hurricane would whip up on the west side, then get caught in the front, and roll back over the town to dump untold inches of rain.

She felt horror inside her, but also the excitement of knowing what was going to happen. There would be flooding. Hurricane Andrew would not continue bending to the right.

Her breath came unevenly, and she had butterflies in her stomach before the ten-o'clock weathercast. For the first time she was going to give a forecast different from the Weather Bureau's prediction for tomorrow. She couldn't yet predict the flooding, but she could give a forerunner forecast.

What if she were wrong? Holly took a deep breath and refused to consider the possibility.

"Tomorrow you're going to see a day of high, thin

overcast clouds," she said when the camera came to her. "Winds will be mostly from the southeast, a little gusty. Showers will begin to develop." Then she really took a deep breath to steady herself as she finished the weathercast. "We're keeping an eye on the front and the hurricane. If the storm comes in our direction, it could join the front about here." She pointed to an area around Wheeler and Shamrock, Texas.

"We must keep in mind at that point, the storm could turn right around and head back our way. In the meantime, we could get torrential amounts of rain."

There! She had done it. Drake might even fire her if he knew how far afield she had gone from the Weather Bureau's forecast.

Drake! No matter how he felt about her, he was always there like a melody in the background of her life. And she must return Kurt's ring.

Such thoughts threatened to keep her awake, but she did sleep. The next morning, it was raining.

Her forecast had been correct!

When she reached the Weather Bureau, tension was high. The wall cloud, which was nothing but pure thunderstorms, could be seen on radar. Originally the wall cloud would have shown up to look like a doughnut, the eye of the hurricane being the hole. But now the eye was disorganized. The storm was getting awfully dry, generating heat and using up moisture.

At the time the hurricane hit the front, it would lose its tropical characteristics and become a huge low-pressure system. Then it would reverse its direction and come back through. As the wall cloud got closer, there would be a massive buildup of low clouds and numerous thunderstorms. The feeder bands would be rotating, creating tremendous amounts of rain. Until the next feeder band came around, winds would die off.

Based on her interpretation of the upper air currents, Holly could now talk to Drake. He must let her go on the air and suggest the evacuation of the low-lying areas of Arrowhead.

It wasn't raining when she left the Weather Bureau to drive to the television station, but the gusts of wind had increased in intensity.

When she reached the television station, Holly knew she had to check the commercial taping schedule. If she had any commercials to do, she would ask Drake to use another announcer.

Only one commercial was on her schedule, but it was one for Denise. *Impossible!* She couldn't do it. Grabbing a handful of charts and notations, she went to Drake's office.

"I will not spend hours putting on clown makeup, wearing a clown suit, and videotaping Denise's shopping-center commercial," she said.

"Whoa, slow down," Drake said calmly. "What's the problem?"

"Problem? You want to know the problem?" Holly shoved her charts in front of him. "Here!"

Drake looked puzzled.

"We're in for rain," she said. "Lots of rain! Within twenty-four hours we could get fifteen inches. The entire area will be completely boggy, and the creeks are going to be overbank full at that point."

"It appears you have your forecast pretty well together, so what's the point in your not doing the commercial?" Drake asked.

"That's not all," she almost wailed, desperation making her voice quiver. "We won't be through with the storm then. It will come right back to Arrowhead, and many parts of the town will be flooded."

"How do you know?" he asked, his hazel eyes quietly studying her.

"I just know," she said stubbornly. "And we'll need to watch for tornadoes in those feeder bands, too. When the other side of the wall cloud hits, winds will come directly east and very strong. Then everything will be calm for a time before the wind changes direction and blows directly west."

"If I let you go on the air with this forecast, you'd better be right." He scowled.

"I know," she said almost prayerfully.

If she should be wrong, she would lose her job and Drake would never speak to her again. She couldn't bear to think about that possibility. For a moment, she was tempted to back down. But she knew she couldn't. Her feelings were too strong. This was her chance, maybe the only chance she'd ever have, to give some meaning to her parents' death.

Shaking from her own emotion and Drake's penetrating gaze, she said, "I'll just have to take my chances!"

Did she see approval in Drake's eyes? She couldn't be sure.

"Go ahead with your work. I'll tell Denise you

won't be doing any more commercials until this weather crisis is over." He glanced at his watch. "How soon can you be ready with our initial warning?"

"Give me thirty minutes," she said.

"At two-thirty, then, we'll interrupt regular programming for the weather bulletin. Keep it as short as possible, but cover the story."

"Yes, sir!" she said crisply, giving him a military salute. Had he really said "*our* initial warning"?

"Holly . . ." Drake called to her as she was leaving.

She turned to face him again. What was flickering in the depth of his eyes?

"I want you to know I admire and respect your courage—your guts—and right or wrong, the station will stand behind you."

It was unbelievable that she wouldn't have to go out on a limb alone. Excitement raced through her. How glad she was that she hadn't weakened and tried to get Henry to agree with her sixth sense.

Knowing full well the seriousness of the weather situation, she was calmer by the time she reached her office. It wasn't long after, though, when she heard a commotion in the hall, the sound of rapid footsteps, then a sharp slap.

"Why did you slap me?" It was Nelson's voice. He sounded hurt, almost pleading.

"Now, I have a question for you. Why do you follow me around? Constantly, interfering with my life! Can't you understand that I want nothing to do with you?" Denise's voice was icy and angry.

"But, Denise, I just want to—"

"I don't care what you want. If you ever interfere between Drake and me again, I'll kill you."

"I've done lots of things for you," Nelson said almost humbly. "Things you don't even know about."

"I mean it, Nelson, if you ever so much as speak to me again, I'll get you fired."

"You'd do that?" Nelson still sounded humble, but incredulous.

Apparently they parted, because Holly heard no more. *Thank goodness*, Holly thought. It was almost time for the weather bulletin. Whatever had Nelson done to cause Denise to talk to him like that? It was a cruel thing to do when Nelson obviously adored her. Henry had certainly been right when he said that this kind of weather made people half-mean.

After the weather bulletin, the switchboard was busy with one call after another. There were telephone calls from churches, owners of buildings, and individuals offering housing for people who wanted to evacuate. Even moving companies and furniture stores called to offer trucks to move possessions and furniture to higher ground. How good people were!

Holly felt the glow of doing something worthwhile as she continued her work. But when the storm was all over and her job settled back into routine, how could she face not having Drake's love?

19

〰〰〰〰〰〰

The first thunderstorms hit the following day. Gusts of wind as high as ninety miles per hour knocked out power lines and uprooted trees. KOK-TV lost its power, but was telecasting again within an hour.

Tornadoes were spotted frequently. Holly was on the air with weather bulletins almost hourly. Luckily, none of the tornadoes hit the ground.

Between each thunderstorm, the wind would die down and there was a stillness that could almost be heard. Then, when the rain started again, the wind had changed its direction. As creeks filled to capacity and the ground became saturated with water, evacuations from Arrowhead's low-lying areas continued. How grateful Holly was that Fran's property, Henry's, and Wimberly Hills were high enough to escape probable flooding. Channel 33 should be safe, too.

Kurt sponsored a number of the weather bulletins, and each time she saw the doll commercial, she thought about his ring in her purse. But she was surprised when he walked into her office late in the afternoon.

His eyes went immediately to her ringless left

hand. "I almost knew," he said, his gray eyes somber. "It just didn't work, did it?"

"I'm sorry," she said. She must have been more tired than she knew, because tears filled her eyes.

"It's okay," he said when she handed him the ring. "But there's more than your work keeping us apart. It's Wimberly, isn't it?"

She looked at him, feeling miserable but unable to deny the truth of his statement.

"You take care of yourself," he said. "As for me, if you're right about the flooding, downtown will get its share of water. I'll be busy for a while with operation mop-up."

When Kurt left, there was no chance to brood. It was time for the six-o'clock news run. She wished she could have given a more cheerful forecast, but there was a good feeling, too, that if nature was going on a rampage, she had been given the opportunity to make it less costly in lives and property.

She had finished eating a tuna sandwich at her desk when Drake came in. It was the first time she had seen him all day. He walked around her desk and sat on the edge of it facing her.

"Such a big job you're doing for such a little girl," he said, and brushed his hand across her cheek. "You need sleep, my love."

My love. Oh, if he only meant that. He was only being kind. "I'll sleep when this is over," she said.

"You'll sleep tonight after the ten-o'clock news," he said firmly. "After this weather is over, I want you to take a few days off and rest."

Holly did go home immediately after the late

weathercast, driving slowly in the rain and trying to avoid patches of high water along the way.

But once in bed, sleep wouldn't come. Her head was spinning with questions. Had Drake noticed she wasn't wearing Kurt's ring? How could she work with him day after day, loving him without hope for the future? Wouldn't it be better if she could dry up like the ground would, and feel nothing?

She must have gone to sleep with that feeling, because she awoke with an emptiness inside her. As she looked out at the sheets of rain coming down, she felt guilty that she had slept at all. She should have stayed with her job. With rain coming down this way, flooding had surely begun. But of course, weather would be the big news now, and the entire news department would be on the story.

Hurriedly she showered and dressed in blue jeans, her comfortable terry top, and boots. In case she didn't have time to get back home and change, she took clothes with her for the six-o'clock weather.

Water was too high on the boulevard route she usually took, so she had to circle around several blocks to find her way to the television station. From the car radio she had learned the flooding was bad. Boats were out checking to see if there were any families who hadn't already evacuated the flooded areas.

It was slow going, but at last she pulled the Sunbird into the parking area of the television station. Through the glass doors she saw Nelson Sternum with a camera in his hand.

Inside the door, she shook the water from her umbrella and said hello.

This was a different Nelson than she'd ever seen before. He looked friendly and even smiled at her.

"I thought you might like to go with me to shoot footage in the flooded areas," he said. "You could pick up some interesting sidelights for your weathercast."

She was tempted to go, but she hesitated, wondering if she should.

"Drake says it's okay," Nelson said.

"In that case, I'd love to," she replied. "Let me check the weather wire and I'll be right with you."

There were more reports of flooding on the wire stories, but really nothing new. Even though it was several hours before she was due to report for work, she stopped at the control room and told Bryan she was going out to shoot film with Nelson.

When they drove away from the television station, the rain had almost stopped. Holly hoped devoutly that it was almost over and that by tomorrow the floodwaters would begin to recede.

It wasn't until they were half a mile away that Nelson spoke. "I lied to you," he said. "I didn't ask Drake about taking you along, but I had to talk with you away from the television station."

Alarmed, Holly remembered Nelson's strange behavior on the way home from the Wichitas. She must stay calm. "It would be best if you take me back."

"I must tell you something," he said. "Please, listen to me."

Obviously she had no choice. "What do you want to say?"

"I . . . I never meant to hurt you," he said.

"Hurt me?" she echoed.

"The notes, the weathercock," he said. "I took the doll, too."

"But you brought the doll back," Holly said. What on earth was going on?

"I put it back when I realized it was valuable and how much it meant to your grandmother." He spoke very low.

Holly turned her gaze on him and saw a shamed look on his face. She said, "You made the phone calls, too?"

He nodded.

"But why?"

"It's complicated, and I went a little crazy," his voice was trembling.

She waited for him to compose himself. Finally he continued. "First, I'm Jim Carstairs' nephew. I've idolized him since I was a little kid. I hated Drake for firing him."

"That has nothing to do with me," Holly said.

"I know," he admitted, "but I got all mixed up. When you came to work, I thought you were a danger to Denise. She acted like you were, too."

"But that concerned her feelings for Drake, not my work."

"I know that now." Nelson stared at the wheel. "I thought, too, that if I could get rid of you, that would hurt Drake. It all got mixed up together—you, Drake, Uncle Jim, and Denise."

"I'm sorry, I had forgotten that—"

"The way I felt about Denise?" Nelson asked. "Can you understand loving someone, but only wanting what's best for them?"

For a moment she was stunned by his question. Did she love Drake enough to be glad if it was Denise who could make him happy? She would think about that later, but now she forced her thoughts back to Nelson. "I couldn't help but hear you and Denise yesterday," Holly said. "Why was she so angry with you?"

He smiled ruefully. "I really blew it there. But I think it brought me completely back to sanity." Nelson paused. "I told her she should quit using her female charms on Drake, and try brains instead. Crazy, huh?"

Holly couldn't help but laugh.

They had reached the flooded area now, and Nelson stopped the station wagon above the water's edge. They could hear the water's roar, rushing onward in raging torrents. Two-story houses were covered above the first level and the single-story ones almost to the rooftops. How grateful she was that the warnings had come in time for the occupants to get out. But the cleanup would be dreadful.

Nelson reached behind them for his camera. He said, "I'm sure I'll lose my job over this, but I feel better for having told you."

"No real harm has been done," she consoled. "I'm sure Drake will be willing to forget it."

But just then the station-wagon door flew open. Drake grabbed Nelson by the front of his shirt and pulled him from the car. The camera tumbled toward Holly.

"Wait!" she cried.

"Are you all right?" Drake asked, still holding Nelson by the front of his shirt.

"Of course I'm all right," she said. "He's not dangerous. Turn him loose."

Drake shoved Nelson away, strode toward Holly. She was already out of the car when he reached her, caught her roughly in his arms, pulling her close.

"If anything had happened . . . When Bryan said you'd gone off with Nelson, I was scared stiff!" He gave her a little shake and laughed brokenly. "Right now, I don't think I'll ever let you out of my sight again."

He kissed her, long and deeply. She couldn't tell if the roar was from the rushing water or her own heart. Breathlessly she murmured, "I'll explain later, but please don't fire Nelson."

Turning, Drake told the amazed cameraman to get on with his job, then tucked Holly into the Ramcharger. They didn't go anywhere, though. He sighed, as if letting go a burden of worry, and suddenly smiled as he took Holly's hands.

"From the way Kurt and Denise were eyeing each other at the station, they're considering a merger that goes a lot further than business."

"I'm glad," Holly managed to say.

"So what about us?" Drake demanded. "Would you like to use those days off you have coming for a honeymoon?"

Her heart seemed to turn over before it righted itself and began dancing. "I'll even try to arrange some nice weather," she promised.

Then his mouth came down on hers and she forgot all about what the weather might be outside.

SIGNET Books by Glenna Finley